Zombies in the House

Jake Lancing lives in Somerset. When not writing about adventure-seeking, football-playing angels, he spends his time avoiding work, listening to very uncool music, growing his hair and helping the government to catch spies.* He jumped out of a plane once because it seemed like a good idea at the time.

* One of these things might not be *entirely* true.

PUFFIN BOOKS

Books by Jake Lancing

DEMON DEFENDERS:
CLASSROOM DEMONS

DEMON DEFENDERS:
ZOMBIES IN THE HOUSE

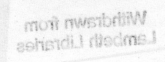

Zombies in the House

JAKE LANCING

PUFFIN

With special thanks to David J. Gatward

PUFFIN BOOKS

Published by the Penguin Group
Penguin Books Ltd, 80 Strand, London WC2R ORL, England
Penguin Group (USA) Inc., 375 Hudson Street, New York, New York 10014, USA
Penguin Group (Canada), 90 Eglinton Avenue East, Suite 700, Toronto,
Ontario, Canada M4P 2Y3 (a division of Pearson Penguin Canada Inc.)
Penguin Ireland, 25 St Stephen's Green, Dublin 2, Ireland
(a division of Penguin Books Ltd)
Penguin Group (Australia), 250 Camberwell Road, Camberwell, Victoria 3124, Australia
(a division of Pearson Australia Group Pty Ltd)
Penguin Books India Pvt Ltd, 11 Community Centre, Panchsheel Park,
New Delhi – 110 017, India
Penguin Group (NZ), 67 Apollo Drive, Rosedale, North Shore 0632, New Zealand
(a division of Pearson New Zealand Ltd)
Penguin Books (South Africa) (Pty) Ltd, 24 Sturdee Avenue,
Rosebank, Johannesburg 2196, South Africa

Penguin Books Ltd, Registered Offices: 80 Strand, London WC2R ORL, England

puffinbooks.com

First published 2009
I

Text copyright © Hothouse Fiction Ltd, 2009
All rights reserved

Set in 13.5/18.75pt Bembo by Palimpsest Book Production Limited,
Grangemouth, Stirlingshire
Made and printed in England by Clays Ltd, St Ives plc

British Library Cataloguing in Publication Data
A CIP catalogue record for this book is available from the British Library

ISBN: 978-0-141-32459-3

www.greenpenguin.co.uk

For Elijah

Contents

1

Alex's Patented Demon Tester

'I'm hungry.'

'And such news is supposed to surprise me how, exactly?'

'Leave it, Spit. You know House can't help himself.'

'On the contrary, Alex. Where food's involved, he's *more* than capable of helping himself.'

Big House, Spit, Alex, Inchy and Cherry were strolling through the garden on a glorious summer's day. Like everything else at number 92 Eccles Road, the garden was obsessively neat. Flower beds marched in precise, orderly rows

1

across a lawn that looked as if it had been trimmed with nail scissors. Large bushes stood dotted around, each one cut into an unlikely military shape, including a tank, an aircraft carrier and a very realistic cavalry charge. There wasn't so much as a leaf out of place.

The same couldn't be said of their destination – a tired old shed tucked away behind a thick hedge, almost as if the house couldn't bear to look at it. The shed was completely out of keeping with the rest of the garden, and its owner had clearly forgotten about it. The windows were cracked and mouldy, the door hung off one hinge and the roof looked like it was about to collapse into a dusty, rotting heap.

It certainly wasn't the sort of place you'd expect to find five young angels.

As the gang slipped inside, Inchy – wearing huge glasses and clothes that would only fit him properly if he doubled in size – looked at Alex expectantly.

'Well then, what is it you're so desperate to show us?'

Alex's blond hair flared in the sunlight blazing through the shed's broken window as he slowly produced a bag from behind his back. It was embroidered with the words *Lucky Dip*.

'Oh no,' said Spit. 'Not that.'

The others looked equally unimpressed. They had all learned to fear Alex's Lucky Dip, the bag of stuff he collected to help him carry out pranks and generally get himself — and them — into deep trouble.

'Behold!' said Alex grandly, reaching into the bag. 'Alex's Patented Demon Tester!'

With a flourish, he pulled out a long pole that seemed far too big ever to have fitted inside. Dangling from one end was a large squarish lump that dripped slightly.

'It's really simple,' Alex grinned.

'Much like its inventor, then,' sniffed Spit, flicking his black hair out of his eyes with a twist of his head.

Ignoring Spit, Alex continued, encouraged by the wide grin slapped across House's face like a colourful sticker.

'This bit here,' he said proudly, pointing at the lump, 'is an ice cube.'

Unable to help himself, Spit interrupted again.

'Really? An ice cube? Are we having a party? Though one whole ice cube is spoiling us, don't you think? Surely half would do.' He sank back against the side of the shed and sighed. 'Could someone let me know when I'm supposed to take this at all seriously?'

Suddenly, Spit found himself suspended two metres in the air.

'Here's the thing,' said House, gazing up at Spit as he held him effortlessly above his head with one hand. 'Alex has an idea that could tell us if someone is a demon. I think that's pretty cool. But more importantly, the quicker he tells us all about it, the quicker we can have lunch. Got it?'

Spit opened his mouth to argue, but House got in first.

'I said, *got it*?'

Spit nodded, though his fiery eyes bored angrily into House as the hefty angel put him back down on the floor.

'Nice move,' said Cherry, the only girl in the gang and the only one with multi-coloured hair. The others had learned that Cherry's ever-changing hair colour and her 'interesting' fashion choices (today she was wearing a stripy shirt, ripped combats, a necktie for a belt, and walking boots) were *never* to be laughed at. Laughing at Cherry was not a good idea. Being a trainee Cherub, she came armed with bow and arrows designed to make people fall in love, and everyone remembered the time when she'd used them on Alex and a donkey. They'd all learned a lesson that day. Especially the donkey.

House sat down, a smug grin on his face. Alex looked at him, impressed.

'You know, you've changed since being kicked out of Cloud Nine Academy.'

'We all have,' replied Spit. 'Our wings were taken away, remember? And we were sent down to Earth. All thanks to you and your stupid pranks.'

'True,' said Alex, 'but if it hadn't been for my stupid pranks, we wouldn't have been here to save Green Hill from Mr Dante, would we?'

Just the mention of the name was enough to make House shudder. Mr Dante had been a Level Four Fire Demon, cunningly disguised as a geography teacher at Green Hill School. Only a few weeks earlier, the gang had foiled his plot to hatch a demon egg in the school cellars.

'Didn't do us much good, though, did it?' said House mournfully. 'I mean, all the evidence was destroyed along with Dante, so we can't prove it ever happened – and we're still stuck down here.'

'But we know that Dante said there were other demons in town,' continued Alex, 'so we need to find out who they are.'

Cherry sighed. 'Why? You seem to be forgetting one teeny-weeny thing, Alex. We're not demon hunters.'

'She's right, Alex,' added Inchy. 'We're not down here to fight the powers of darkness. We're *supposed* to be learning how to be well behaved, so that Gabriel will let us back into Heaven.'

'Precisely!' beamed Spit. 'We should be keeping our heads down and our noses clean, not looking around for more trouble.'

Alex looked deflated for a moment. Then he rallied.

'OK, but just say we *accidentally* stumble on another demon, like we did with Dante. We'll need to be able to prove that it's a demon, right? Which is where my Patented Demon Tester comes in.'

'I give up!' said Cherry. 'Go on, then. Tell us all about it. But if it lands us in trouble, you'll have me to answer to.'

'We were up to "ice cube",' muttered Spit.

'Right, yes,' said Alex, pleased. 'As you can see, the ice cube is attached to *this*.'

Alex wiggled the long pole in his hand.

'Looks like a fishing rod,' observed Inchy.

'It is.'

'And I think I recognize it,' said Inchy. 'Doesn't it belong to –'

'Never mind that,' interrupted Alex. 'Let me show you how it works. Follow me!'

Leading the gang back into the garden, Alex clenched the Demon Tester firmly in his hands. 'Right. Imagine that bush over there is a demon.'

'What bush?' said House.

'The one that looks like Gabriel,' replied Alex, grinning. 'With a big nose and double chin!'

The gang chuckled. The strict Head Angel of Cloud Nine Academy had never been their favourite person, but ever since he had sent them down to Earth without their wings, he'd become even less popular.

Alex coughed to get their attention again.

'So, anyway, that bush over there is a demon, or someone we suspect might be one. And we're here with my Demon Tester.'

'The excitement is killing me,' said Spit sarcastically.

'I could help it out, if you want,' retorted Cherry.

'Are any of you interested in this?' asked Alex exasperatedly. The gang reluctantly turned to watch. 'As I was saying – bush, demon, Demon Tester, OK?'

Everyone nodded.

'Right. Now all I do is *this*.'

With a tremendous flourish, Alex flicked the rod back and cast it forward. The ice cube at the end of the line shot off at lightning speed.

It missed the bush. By miles. And then continued towards the house.

'I wonder when it'll stop,' mused Inchy.

From the other side of the garden, a dull thud and an agonized cry answered his question.

'Oh no,' said Alex.

★ ★ ★

'So let me get this straight,' said Cherry, pointing a bleach-covered toothbrush aggressively at Alex. 'You froze a big block of ice round a fishing hook.'

She was standing in the kitchen, wearing overalls and a scowl that looked particularly out of place on her rosy Cherubic features.

'Yep,' replied Alex.

'And how is that supposed to tell us if someone is a demon?'

'Well,' said Alex, 'demons are hot, right? So if we dangle an ice cube over someone's head and it melts, then we know he or she's a demon, don't we? Genius!'

'Genius? Really?'

Before Alex could say 'Yep' again, Cherry jumped across the room and tried to stick the toothbrush up his left nostril.

'And at what point did your sponge of a brain decide that the best thing to use to create your Demon Tester was Tabbris's prize fishing rod? Did you really think he wouldn't notice? Well? *Well?*'

Cherry's rosy cheeks were more like scarlet now.

'It almost worked, didn't it?' said Alex, backing away. 'I mean, the ice cube really flew through the air, didn't it?'

'He's got a point,' added Inchy. 'It was a very good cast, especially considering he's never done any fishing.'

'Exactly!' said Alex. 'Now imagine if I had some practice. I'd be able to detect a demon from miles away!'

'Mind you,' House ventured in the unimpressed silence that followed, 'the look on Tabbris's face as that ice cube flew towards him –'

'When it actually hit him,' chortled Inchy, 'right on the nose –'

'Just before the ice smashed and the hook caught in his moustache!' Spit laughed out loud. 'It really was pure genius!'

'Well, it *almost* worked,' said Alex rather glumly. 'How was I to know Tabbris would walk out of the house at that very moment? And if he *had* been a demon we'd have known instantly.'

'If Tabbris had been a demon, we'd have got off lightly,' snapped Cherry. 'A demon wouldn't have us cleaning the kitchen from top to bottom with these!'

'*Ow!*' Alex scowled as he tried to rub away the bruise on his arm where the grubby toothbrush had this time found its target.

A firm voice cut into the moment like the sound of a flag snapping in the wind.

'Something the matter?'

The gang turned to see a slight figure standing in the kitchen doorway. He was resting on a cane but it did nothing to diminish his presence. Retired Guardian Angel Major Tabbris was supervising them while they were on Earth, and while he may have looked a bit past it, the gang knew the old angel was a force to be reckoned with. They each quickly shook their head.

'Good,' said Tabbris. 'Then might I suggest that the best way to complete your task is to stop arguing and get on with it. If you work together for once, it shouldn't take you more than five or six hours.'

With that, he turned and left as silently as he'd arrived.

'For an angel he's pretty cranky,' said Inchy.

'Good job I didn't ask him for a sandwich, then,' replied House.

'Come on, guys,' said Alex brightly. 'Let's get this done.'

With that, Inchy and Spit turned to scrub the floor, while Alex, Cherry and House worked together to attack the sink. They continued in silence for what seemed like forever, each of them getting more and more exhausted.

'Are we still on for footie practice tomorrow?' asked Alex finally, hoping to lift team spirits with the mention of their favourite hobby. Instead, all he got was a tired 'Uh-huh' from his friends.

'Not exactly the response I was after.'

'Would you prefer it if we all threw these toothbrushes at you to emphasize our enthusiasm?' asked Spit.

Cherry jumped in hastily before Spit and Alex could get into one of their usual arguments.

'You reckon we've got a chance to qualify for the county five-a-side, then, do you?'

Alex nodded. 'Of course! What've we got to lose?'

'Our self-respect?' said Spit. 'Don't you remember how we got hammered by The Black Crows at school?'

'We weren't used to Earth's gravity, that's all,'

replied Alex. '*And* we were a man down. But we were awesome at the Academy, weren't we? There's no reason we can't be just as good here on Earth. All we need is a bit more practice.'

The gang looked unconvinced as House pulled his head out of the oven and announced through a grease-streaked face that it was finished.

'Perfect timing,' came Tabbris's voice again.

'Oh, er . . . Hi, Tabbris,' said Alex. 'We didn't hear you come in.'

'Of course you didn't,' Tabbris replied. 'I wouldn't have lasted long in Special Operations if I couldn't get into a room without being heard, would I? Silent and graceful, that's what we are.'

Spit looked at House. 'Didn't you say you wanted to join Spec Ops once you'd qualified as a Guardian Angel?'

House nodded.

'"Silent and graceful"? Well, that rules you out.'

House scowled, but with Tabbris standing by, he swallowed his sharp reply.

'Now, let's see how you've done, shall we?'

The gang held their breath as Tabbris prowled around the kitchen, scrutinizing every centimetre of the floor, walls and surfaces.

'Not bad,' the old angel mused. 'Not bad at all. But I wonder . . .'

And to everyone's horror he suddenly pulled on a pair of white cotton gloves, stuck out a finger and wiped it behind the oven.

'We're dead,' said Inchy.

The gang held their breath.

'Let's have a look,' replied Tabbris, slowly raising his finger to the light.

It was spotless.

'I knew he'd try that,' whispered House, 'so I did double cleaning round the back.'

'Nice one, mate!' grinned Alex.

Tabbris turned to face the gang.

'Well, I have to admit, I'm impressed,' he said.

'Impressed enough to send us home?' asked Spit optimistically.

Tabbris raised one snowy eyebrow. 'Hardly. Let's not forget that you wouldn't have been in this position at all if you hadn't seen fit to steal my fishing rod. You'll need to do something far more impressive if you want to get back to Cloud Nine. Still, you do deserve some reward, I suppose.'

'Please, sir,' piped up Alex. 'Could we be allowed to enter the county five-a-side football tournament, then?'

'If you really feel the need to partake in mindless barbarity, then I suppose you must,' replied Tabbris. 'But I've got something far more fun as well. Community service.'

'Doesn't sound much fun to me,' said House.

Tabbris carried on as if he hadn't heard.

'Gabriel and I have decided that, as part of your whole Earth-bound learning experience, you should try doing some community service. And as next week is half term, you will be visiting patients at Green Hill Hospital every day.'

'Every day? You're joking,' said Cherry before she could stop herself.

'No, I'm not,' Tabbris replied. 'If I was joking I would probably have said, "Did you hear the one about five silly young angels who didn't know how to behave and had to be sent to Earth to learn a thing or two from an old angel who was too kind for his own good?"'

Tabbris chuckled at his own unfunny joke. He was the only one.

'You will visit the patients in the hospital, practise

your listening skills and get a better understanding of what makes humans tick. Which is essential if you're ever to become *proper* angels.'

'Sounds utterly marvellous,' said Spit, without an ounce of warmth in his voice.

'Indeed it is,' beamed Tabbris. 'And if you do it properly and without getting into trouble, then I will allow you to play in this football tournament. Although I think that you'll enjoy your community service a lot more than kicking a ball around a piece of grass, wouldn't you agree?'

No one dared reply.

2
Star Attraction

'We don't play against girls.'

Cherry raised her eyebrows and looked at the person who'd just spoken, the leader of the group of boys she'd just invited to have a friendly kickabout. After hours spent scrubbing the kitchen yesterday, her body ached so much she'd hardly slept. Now the gang were down at the local recreation ground for some footie practice, and she wasn't in the mood for any mickey-taking.

'Scared we'll beat you?'

The boy smirked.

'Yeah, whatever,' he said, looking at the rest of his mates. 'Like any team that plays with a chick is ever going to have a chance against us. Why don't you just go back home and mess around with your make-up or cry over some boy band, saddo!'

Alex noticed Cherry's cheeks darken. This boy didn't know just how much danger he was in. Cherry stepped forward, eyeballing him. Now they were face-to-face, almost nose-to-nose.

'Hey, look,' said the boy, standing his ground, 'this girl thinks she's something!'

The other boys laughed.

Cherry smiled coldly. 'What's your name?'

'Why should I tell you?'

'It'll make it easier when I call the ambulance.'

'OK,' he said, 'if you think you're so special, let's play, bogey hair! My name's Skally, and we'll go easy on you, OK? Don't want you having to go home boo-hoo-hooing to mumsie-wumsie-woos!'

This got a huge laugh from the rest of the boys as Skally strutted back to them.

Alex looked at the scowl on Cherry's face. 'You do know Cherubs are supposed to be nice, don't you?' he reminded her.

'I am nice,' snarled Cherry as the rest of the team jogged over. 'I didn't punch an arrow into his butt, did I?'

'We've got about an hour before we have to be at the hospital,' said Alex. 'Looks like it's game on.'

'Then let's go.'

They all watched as Cherry made her way to the centre of the pitch, bouncing the ball slowly and deliberately, her eyes never straying from the boy called Skally.

'Even I've never made her *that* angry,' said Spit. 'I must be losing my touch.'

'Maybe you're just realizing that being part of a team and being nice to people is actually quite a good idea,' said House.

'We're not people; we're angels.'

'Yes,' replied House, 'and we all know what happens when one goes bad, don't we?'

Spit's eyes glinted. 'I'm no Hell's Angel.'

But House was already jogging off to go in goal and didn't hear him. A shout echoed across the field.

'Oi! It's kick-off!'

Waving, Spit turned and started to run out on

to the left wing. And that was when an idea hit him like a power-driven penalty kick.

'Score, Inchy?'

Inchy looked at Alex. 'Three all.' He glanced at his watch and added, 'Five minutes to go. Pity we can't use aerial attack, isn't it?'

Alex smiled, remembering swooping down from the sky to score the goal that won them the Academy tournament. 'I'd give anything for a pair of wings.'

'That makes two of us.'

'We need to win this for Cherry,' said Alex. 'That Skally really upset her.'

'And he hasn't learned his lesson,' replied Inchy. 'Look.'

Alex turned to see Skally and his team all pointing at Cherry and dancing around like ballerinas.

'What are they doing?' asked Alex.

'They're trying to wind her up,' replied Inchy. 'And I think it's working.'

Alex glanced over to where Cherry was standing with Spit, who looked like he was having trouble trying to calm her down. As they watched,

Spit patted her on the back and then sprinted to the edge of the pitch. He bent down, fiddled with something in the pile of jumpers and bags, then headed back to the centre of the pitch.

'What's he up to?' asked Alex.

'Dunno,' said Inchy. 'Tightening his studs?'

Before Alex had time to wonder why Spit would be messing around with his boots in the middle of a match, a stray pass landed right at his own feet. He glanced up to see two of the other team steaming towards him. Instinct took over and he dummied a left, then skipped to the right, leaving one of the boys stranded. But the other was still on him.

'Alex, switch it!'

Across the pitch, Alex caught sight of Cherry, arms waving. Without a second thought, he chipped the ball to her, high over the head of his marker.

Unfortunately, Cherry was still so angry that the power behind her first touch sent the ball careering in completely the wrong direction. House leapt into the air and only just managed to save an own goal. Cherry let out a shriek of frustration and annoyance.

'Corner!' yelled Skally. '*Corner!*'

With only seconds left, the other team, including their goalie, raced down the pitch for the corner, laughing at Cherry.

Alex rushed over to join Inchy in defence, but where was Spit? For a moment, Alex couldn't see him, but then he spotted him among the opposing players, bumping up against them and jostling each one in turn. What *was* he doing?

Skally took the corner and Alex didn't have time to think about Spit's strange behaviour any more.

The ball rose high. Alex started to follow it, but as he did so, he noticed something odd. The opposing players hadn't moved at all. They were just standing there staring at each other with rather daft smiles on their faces.

'House!' he called. 'What's going on?'

'Don't know,' said House, as the ball landed just in front of one of the opposition, giving him a clear shot at goal. Still the boy didn't move. Instead, he seemed to be gazing at House with the kind of eyes you'd only use on someone you were about to ask out.

'Mine!' yelled Alex, racing up to the ball and sending a pass downfield towards Spit. Alex turned to chase it, only to find himself face-to-face with a second boy from the other team. The boy smiled soppily.

'I love you, man.'

'What?'

'I mean, I *really* love you!'

The boy stepped forward to hug Alex, who nearly tripped on his bootlaces as he tried to back off. Struggling to keep his balance, he bumped into two more members of the opposition. But they were too busy hugging each other to notice.

'You're my best friend,' one of them sighed, and burst into tears.

'What's going on?' shouted Alex. 'What on *Earth* is happening?'

The only answer he got was a pointing finger from Inchy.

Alex turned to see Spit slot a perfect pass to a figure racing down the right wing. Alex couldn't believe his eyes.

'It's Cherry!' he shouted.

She had the ball at her feet and a clear pitch

ahead. She was even onside. All she had to do was shoot. But someone else had also seen her.

'No!' screamed Skally, belting away from the corner. 'No!'

But Alex knew Skally didn't have a chance. Cherry was already past the halfway line. With a satisfying thump, she unleashed a powerful shot and the ball slammed into the back of the net.

Skally stopped dead, despair sticking him to the ground. The rest of his team hadn't even noticed. They were still far too busy hugging each other and crying uncontrollably.

Alex surveyed the scene. 'Something's not right here.'

Then Cherry started dancing and singing.

'We're the winners, we're the winners, we're the best!
You're the losers, you're the losers, you're the worst!
And there's no point even trying,
Cos you'll only end up crying!
We're the Winners, you're the Losers, we're the Best!'

Cherry's voice sliced through the air like a razor blade, making the goalposts shake.

'She's not very good, is she?' winced Alex.

'No,' said Inchy, covering his ears as a flock of pigeons plummeted out of the sky, stunned by the sheer awfulness of Cherry's singing. 'Music was never her best subject. Don't you remember why she got kicked out of the Heavenly Chorus?'

'No, why?'

'I was there. When she tried to sing a high C, my harp melted.'

Spit joined them.

'Well, Cherry's certainly happier now, isn't she?' he grinned. 'Serves that lot right, I reckon.'

'What do you mean?' asked Alex suspiciously. Spit was smiling just a little *too* smugly. 'What did you do?'

'I helped Cherry score the winning goal, that's what. And it was a top pass, I think you'll agree.'

'That's not all, though, is it?'

'Such mistrust,' protested Spit. 'Can't you just let Cherry enjoy the victory? Or are you upset that it wasn't you who scored the winning goal?' he added slyly.

'Come off it. You did something, didn't you? I mean, people don't just start hugging each other for no reason, do they?'

'Humans can be happy,' protested Cherry. 'It *is* allowed.'

'But this is football!' said Alex, raising his voice. 'Footballers don't hug each other in the middle of a match. Not unless they've scored.'

Just then, Skally rushed up and shoved Cherry so hard she almost fell over.

'What did you do to them? You cheated! You stupid girl – you cheated, didn't you?'

House stepped in. 'Back off, pal.'

Skally opened his mouth, but at the sight of Big House looming over him, he thought twice about saying anything else. Instead, he spat on the ground and ran back to his team, who were now walking away from the pitch arm in arm, singing 'Always Look on the Bright Side of Life' in perfect harmony.

'And footballers certainly don't do *that*,' said Alex.

'No, you're right,' said Spit. 'I wasn't expecting that, either.'

'So you *did* do something! I knew it!'

'Actually, it was rather clever. You should be pleased.'

'Yes, you should,' said Cherry. 'It was a great pass!'

'No, not that,' smirked Spit. 'What I did with your arrow.'

'What?'

'Well,' explained Spit, 'I didn't like the way those guys were taking the mickey out of you. I could see that you wanted to beat them really badly, and I wanted to help, you know. So when I went over to the bags, I snapped the point off one of your arrows. Then, when I bumped up against those guys, I gave them each a tiny nick with it, just enough to confuse them. I wasn't after any falling-in-love-with-a-donkey stuff, just a distraction, that's all. And it worked, didn't it? Cherry scored, we won and they've learned a lesson. And the effects of the arrow will wear off in an hour or so.'

'So we didn't win,' said Cherry, her voice low and sad. 'We cheated.'

'I was just trying to help,' said Spit, sounding suddenly deflated. 'I thought you'd be pleased. Looking out for the team and all that. You know, like you said at the kick-off, House. One for all and all for one?'

House shook his head sadly. Alex stepped forward.

'Spit, mate, I get *why* you did it. None of us liked seeing Cherry upset and angry. But the way you tried to help . . . it just wasn't right.'

'Yeah,' snarled Spit, 'but it would've been OK if you'd done it, wouldn't it? Then it would have been a "genius plan".'

'No, it wouldn't,' said Alex.

Cherry approached Spit and placed a hand on his arm. 'Thanks,' she said, 'but next time, try something a little less unfair, OK?'

Spit opened his mouth, but before he could reply, Inchy gasped.

'Oh no!'

'What's up?' asked House.

Inchy showed everyone his watch. 'We're late!'

'Tabbris will kill us if he finds out,' groaned Alex. 'Let's go!'

Without another word, Alex, House, Inchy and Cherry ran to grab their bags, leaving Spit to ponder whether the life of a Hell's Angel would be so bad after all.

'That's convenient,' said Spit, nodding at a tired rusty gate bearing a sign that said *Green Hill Cemetery*. 'Right next to the hospital.'

'Not very comforting for the patients, is it?' said Inchy.

'Why not?' asked House.

Spit looked at him disbelievingly.

'Humans don't like death,' explained Alex. 'The dead scare them.'

'Yeah, well what scares me is the thought of what Tabbris will do to us when he finds out we've missed visiting hours,' snapped Cherry.

'Maybe we should just go home and pretend that we've been visiting,' suggested House. 'I mean, how would Tabbris know we're not telling the truth?'

'We can't just lie,' retorted Alex. 'Besides, this is Tabbris we're talking about – he's got spies everywhere. He's probably best friends with the chief nurse or something.'

'I hate to interrupt,' said Inchy, 'but look!'

The gang turned. Just ahead of them stood the entrance to Green Hill Hospital, a big building with so many windows it looked like a giant glitter ball. And outside the main doors stood a large crowd of expectant-looking people, all wearing dressing gowns.

'They look like patients,' said Alex incredulously.

'What are they waiting outside for?' asked Cherry.

'That?' said Inchy, pointing towards a huge car, so black it seemed to distort light as it drove past. As it pulled up outside the hospital, the crowd went wild.

'Look,' said Cherry, edging forward, 'someone's getting out.'

And someone was – but the figure that stepped from the car looked immediately too big ever to have been in it. His tall frame towered over the crowd of screaming patients. As he swung round theatrically, arms outstretched, sunlight blazed off so many rings, bangles, bracelets and necklaces that it was like a laser light show. But everything else about the man – from his shoulder-length hair and eyeliner, right down to his tight jeans and leather shoes – was black. He was like a shadow speckled with diamonds, or a dash of the starry night sky gone walkabout in the day.

'I'm guessing he's not a doctor,' said Inchy.

Then the figure spoke.

'My deepest heartfelt thanks, everyone. Really, this is just too much, far too much. I am humbled by your adoration. I just hope I can live up to your love. Everything I do, I do it . . . for you!'

The crowd screamed even louder, almost as if they half expected a guitar solo.

'They do rather like him, don't they?' said Spit, as the patients at the front of the crowd started begging for autographs on everything from plaster casts to eye patches.

'They do,' replied Alex suspiciously. 'And they seem very enthusiastic for people who are supposed to be ill.'

The strange black-clad man proceeded slowly into the hospital, security guards keeping the patients at arm's length. Occasionally he would turn and hug one of the crowd, or say, 'Bless you, bless you all.'

Finally, just as he was about to pass through the doors, he turned and, with a flick of his wrist, cast out a spray of what looked like oversized confetti. One bit landed near Cherry and she picked it up.

'What is it?' asked Inchy, craning his neck to see.

Cherry shrugged and showed them a rather soft-focus photograph of the man they'd just seen enter the hospital. It was signed *Aubrey Adonis – Hospital DJ* in big loopy handwriting.

A nearby patient spotted the gang looking at the picture and came over.

'Isn't he just the most beautiful person?' she gushed. 'So loving and gentle and kind and fabulous . . .'

For a moment, it looked like the woman would never stop. But then she seemed suddenly overcome by the situation and abruptly fainted into the arms of a stunningly pretty nurse. The nurse didn't seem at all surprised, but simply shot the gang a beaming smile and carried the unconscious woman back into the hospital.

'Aubrey Adonis?' said House. 'What kind of name is that?'

It was then Alex used the smile everyone dreaded. The one that generally came fully armed with plenty of ways to get them into big, big trouble. The one he usually followed by saying 'I've got a plan' or 'Let's go and find out'.

'I've got a plan,' said Alex. 'Let's go and find out!'

3
The Happy Ward

'Are you sure this is a good idea, Alex?' asked Inchy as the gang marched in through the automatic doors. 'I'm not sure we're allowed to go inside now visiting time's over.'

'I'm sure nobody will mind,' said Alex dismissively. 'The patients must be bored with people always visiting at the same time. They'll probably be pleased to have a change. Let's split up. If we all go to a different ward, we can see more people. Spread the joy.'

'"Spread the joy"?' echoed Spit. 'You sound like that cheesy Adonis guy.'

'Yeah? Well, we want to find out more about him too, don't we?' replied Alex. 'And look at it this way – the sooner we get this done, the sooner we get home. Let's go.'

Reluctantly, the gang peeled off to go their separate ways.

Five minutes later, Inchy found himself staring up at a sign that said *Geriatric Ward*. Great – he'd got lumbered with the smelly old people. With a sigh, he pulled out the small rosewood box that contained his Scales of Justice. As a Voice of Reason Angel, Inchy used them to judge whether a course of action would turn out well or badly. This time, however, they just hung there, utterly motionless.

'Well,' muttered Inchy, 'at least they're not telling me it's going to be awful.'

Placing the scales carefully back into his pocket, he took a deep breath and walked through the doors, trying to ignore the mental images of lots of wrinkly old people smelling of soup and sweaty slippers and sitting in miserable silence.

'Wa-hey!'

'Ooh, look – a little man to talk to! Brilliant!'

'Wayth a minith while I geth me teeth in!'

'Over here, boy, if you want to hear some stories about the good ol' days!'

Inchy froze, shocked by the riot of noise and movement that greeted him.

'Er, hi.'

Cautiously, he edged forward, more than a little surprised by the warmth of his welcome. He had only taken a couple of steps, though, when an orange bounced off his head.

'Howzat!' waved an old man. 'Sorry! Just practising my fast bowling.'

'You're all . . . happy,' said Inchy, confused. Weren't old people supposed to be gloomy? They were nearly dead, after all.

'Well, of course we're happy, dear!' chirped a voice to his left. 'Hospital is just so much fun!'

Inchy turned to see who'd spoken, only to come face-to-face with a world of wool. The wizened old lady in the nearest bed was wearing a knitted hat, a knitted jumper and knitted blouse. And she was knitting.

'Come here,' she said. 'Now stand there. Good.'

The old lady held up her knitting and placed it against Inchy's chest.

'You know, I think it's the perfect size.'

'It's pink,' said Inchy.

'No, it's not,' said the old lady, 'it's strawberry blush, and don't you forget it.'

'What is it?'

The old lady smiled vacantly for a few seconds, then said, 'You know what? I haven't a clue! Mavis? Mavis!'

Something stirred in a bed some way down the ward.

The old lady held up her knitting and shouted, 'Mavis! What is this I'm knitting? Can you remember?'

'Roast dinner!' came the reply.

'Oh yes, of course. A roast dinner.'

Inchy looked at the old lady, puzzled.

'What?'

'Look,' said the old lady and opened the cupboard by her bed. 'See?'

Inchy gazed in.

'Well, what do you think?' she asked, grinning.

'Er, well,' said Inchy, 'I've, er, well, I've never seen a knitted roast chicken before.'

'No,' said the old lady, 'and neither has anyone else. It's OK, I think, but I'm happier with the roast potatoes.'

'The gravy's very effective,' said Inchy, wondering what he'd ever done to end up discussing knitted food. Whatever Tabbris had said, it seemed a very unlikely way to get back into Heaven.

'Thank you,' said the old lady. 'My name's Lily, by the way. Lily Patton.'

'Pleased to meet you,' said Inchy. 'I'm Inchy.'

He had just worked up enough courage to ask *why* this old lady was knitting a roast dinner, when another voice interrupted.

'Any chance of a souvenir, Lily?'

Inchy turned to find an old man with a sad face standing behind him.

'You leaving us, Harold?'

'Afraid so,' said the old man. 'I've just been discharged. I don't want to go, really.'

'Can't say I blame you. Here.' Lily reached down to her cupboard and handed Harold two knitted roast parsnips and a handful of knitted sprouts. 'I've not done the carrots yet,' she said. 'Sorry.'

'Not to worry,' said Harold, and shuffled back to his own bed, where a half-packed suitcase awaited him.

'I don't get it,' muttered Inchy.

'What, my lad?' said Lily.

'Well, this is a hospital, isn't it? It's not a holiday. I didn't think it was supposed to be fun. Aren't people supposed to *want* to go home?'

Before Lily could answer, a nurse walked in.

'Oooh, this is the best part of the day!' giggled Lily excitedly.

The nurse was smiling like that was all her face was designed for. Her teeth were bright, her eyes wide and she was carrying pompoms. Pink ones with silver sparkles.

'Ladies and gentlemen!' the nurse announced, thrusting the pompoms into the air and bobbing her head. 'It's the moment you've all been waiting for! Live on Green Hill Hospital Radio, Aubrey Adonis is back on the airwaves!'

Inchy pricked up his ears. Maybe this was his chance to find out more about the peculiar-looking DJ.

The nurse stopped bobbing her head, but only so that she could do a couple of spins on the spot. 'So jump into your beds, rattle your tablets and loosen your bandages!'

The nurse's eyes sparkled at each and every patient in the ward. Then, to Inchy's ever-increasing surprise, she ran forward, leapt into the air, did a somersault and landed in the splits. 'It's . . . *Brain Dead*!'

And at those two simple words, the whole ward went wild. The air was suddenly filled with whooping and yelling and false teeth and grapes and then . . .

Silence.

Inchy stared. 'What's going on, Lily?'

Lily didn't respond.

'Lily?'

Inchy looked over to see that she, like everyone else in the ward, was now sitting silently on her bed, wearing a set of heavy-duty earphones and staring into nothingness.

Inchy waved his hand in front of Lily's eyes.

Nothing, not even a blink. The clatter of doors made him turn just in time to catch a glimpse of pompoms disappearing through the doors of the ward. *What* had just happened? He'd never seen or heard of anything like it in his life!

A voice interrupted. 'Hsss! Boy! Hey you!'

Inchy turned. Stared.

'Over here!'

Inchy didn't even have time to work out where the voice was coming from before something whizzed past his ear to *thwack* into the chair at the side of Lily's bed. It was a dart fashioned from a large syringe with flights made from medical prescriptions. A note was wrapped around it.

Inchy opened the note and read, *Over here, you numpty!*

Only then did he notice, off in the darkest corner of the ward, the wildly glinting eyes of an old man with a thin red bandage wrapped round his head.

'Quick!' hissed the old man. 'Before zey all go valkabout again!'

'What do you mean?' said Inchy, running over. 'What's going on?'

The old man saluted smartly.

'Kowalski. Captain,' he said, his voice thick with an accent Inchy didn't recognize. 'Velcome to ze front line, soldier!'

'I'm not a soldier, I'm an ange–' started Inchy,

stopping himself just in time. 'Er, I mean I'm a visitor. How can I help?'

'Look!' said Mr Kowalski, handing him a pair of earphones identical to all the others in the ward. 'See? See vot I did? Zey von't catch me asleep, oh no! I have gone for days vizout sleep. Days, I tell you! Ve Poles, ve are survivors, you know? Nossing can beat us! Nossing can beat me!'

Mr Kowalski thumped a clenched fist against his chest defiantly, and coughed.

Inchy couldn't help but think that Mr Kowalski would probably get on rather well with Tabbris. Then he looked at the headphones and found them stuffed with cotton wool. It looked like Mr Kowalski was a total nut ball. Nuttier than Tabbris, even.

'See?' said Mr Kowalski, eyes wide and wild. 'It von't affect me viz zat stuffed in zere – I'm not going to end up like the rest of zem. Look at zem!'

Mr Kowalski gestured round the ward with an age-spotted hand.

'What?' asked Inchy. 'They're just listening to the radio.'

Mr Kowalski seized Inchy's hand and leaned forward.

'Zat show, *Brain Dead*,' he said. 'Hospital radio show. Zey're all hooked. Addicted. But it's more zan a radio show – much, much more!'

Inchy tried to pull away, but was surprised to find himself held fast by the old man, his grip like iron.

'You heff to tell somebody! Zis hospital . . . Zere is something wrong viz it, something dark and evil!'

'But why can't *you* tell someone?' asked Inchy. 'The nurses?'

'No!' howled Mr Kowalski, his face shocked. 'No, zey are a part of it too. No, it must be someone outside, someone who is not involved. I know too much already. Ze nurses are already suspicious. I cannot leave ze ward. Besides, I have friends in here – I can't just leave zem! You've got to raise ze alarm!'

'I . . . I –' started Inchy.

Mr Kowalski sat up straight and, to Inchy's surprise, lifted him clean off the floor and pulled him so close that their noses almost touched. For a few seconds that seemed to last hours, Mr

Kowalski stared straight into Inchy's face, the whites of his eyes almost glow-in-the-dark bright.

'Don't you understand? Hell is coming, child! *Hell!* Now go!'

Inchy, suddenly released, turned and ran.

In the ward, no one stirred.

4

After Hours

'Watch it!'

'Cherry!' said Inchy, skidding to a halt.

'What's the hurry? What's wrong?'

'This hospital is seriously weird,' said Inchy.

'How do you mean?'

'Well, for a start, no one wants to leave – they're happy here. In fact, they're more than happy, they're ecstatic!'

'You too, then?' said Cherry, falling into step beside Inchy as they headed for the exit.

'What?'

'Well,' said Cherry, 'after what Alex said about

people in hospitals being miserable, I was expecting everyone on my ward to be gloomy, but they were happy as well. It's freaky. We ended up having a sing-song and –'

'You sang?' said Inchy incredulously. 'And they were still happy? People smiled and stuff? Didn't any of them wonder why their ears were bleeding?'

Cherry folded her arms and stared as hard as she could.

'I'm sorry,' said Inchy. 'It's just that happiness wasn't the weirdest thing on my ward.'

'Why? What else happened?'

'Well, for a start, there was this break-dancing nurse. Well, she was more like a cheerleader, actually. And then this radio show came on, *Brain Dead*, and everyone completely zoned out, and then this crazy old guy fires a syringe at me and tells me that the hospital is evil or something. I mean – *Oof!*'

Inchy's tirade was cut off as he and Cherry bumped into something.

'Hey, slow down, little people, OK? Life's fast enough as it is. So why not park a while and, you know, take a rest.'

Stumbling backwards, the pair looked up. Above them, Aubrey Adonis rose in all his skinny-jean-clad glory. As they stared, the DJ crouched down so that he was face-to-face with them.

'Little friends,' he said, as he reached out and pulled them close to him. Adonis was evidently trying to be friendly, but the combination of his bony limbs and the chunky rings on his fingers made it an experience rather like being hugged by a skeleton. The DJ smelled strongly of cheap aftershave, which masked a deeper, earthier smell that was even less pleasant.

'It hurts me to see such young ones in hospital,' he continued. 'I can only hope I am, in some small and insignificant way, able to ease your pain a little.' Adonis's lips parted in a smile that released a stand-up-and-salute row of gold teeth, each embossed with a tiny diamond.

'Yes, well, er, thank you . . .' began Cherry, trying to wriggle free of Adonis's embrace, but only succeeding in getting a mouthful of greasy backcombed hair.

'Here,' said Adonis, standing up, 'perhaps this will help?'

With that, he flicked back his ankle-length

leather coat, whipped out a huge wallet and shook it open. It only stopped unfolding when it hit the floor. Twice. Reaching into the wallet, Adonis pulled from it two pictures of himself holding a lamb and a puppy. Handing them to Cherry and Inchy, he said, 'Whenever you look at these, it will remind you that I'm thinking of you and praying you'll get better.'

The two angels took the pictures, speechless.

'But what are you little dudes doing out of your cosy cribs anyhow?' asked Adonis, his brow furrowed. 'You should be tucked up listening to my show!'

'Oh, we're not patients,' replied Inchy without thinking. 'We're just visit— *Ouch!*'

Inchy broke off as Cherry elbowed him sharply in the ribs. Adonis's frown deepened.

'Visiting hours are over, dudes. You shouldn't be here. Time to go.'

Adonis turned and walked over to a nurse sitting on a chair in a nearby ward. She had *Brain Dead* headphones clamped on to her head and a dreamy expression on her face. Adonis reached out and tore the headphones away in one swift, almost painful, movement. Then he snapped his fingers and the nurse seemed to wake up.

'I found these two wandering the corridors,' he murmured. 'Could you please show them the way out. And maybe you should take more care to make sure all the visitors leave at the end of visiting hours tomorrow.'

'Of course, Mr Adonis. I'm sorry, it won't happen again,' said the nurse. She looked positively ashamed of herself, but Adonis ignored her apology, turning his attention back to Cherry and Inchy.

'Fare thee well, my little friends,' he said, his voice all silk and honey again. 'I go now to bring what little healing I can to those less fortunate than I.'

And with that he glided off down the corridor, leaving Cherry and Inchy to be herded towards the exit by the now very alert, awake and bossy nurse. As she ushered them out of the door, Cherry could see the rest of the gang waiting for them on the other side of the car park. The nurse turned, favoured them with another radiant smile, rustled her pompoms, chanted 'Ooh, yeah, Ad-on-is!', then left with a very impressive backflip.

Inchy turned to Cherry. 'That was really odd.'

'I know,' replied Cherry. 'Those pompoms are hideous.'

'No, not that!' said Inchy. 'Well, not *only* that. You know how we were just talking to Adonis?'

'How could I forget?'

'And you know how everyone was listening to his show on the radio?'

Cherry ground her teeth. 'Get to the point, Inch.'

'Well, how come Adonis is walking around the hospital at the same time he's on the radio?'

'Simple,' said Cherry. 'The show's pre-recorded.'

'But then what on Earth is he doing while the show is on?'

'And then she wanted to play kiss-chase. I'm not joking – *kiss-chase*! And when she caught me . . . Yeurch! Her lips were like wet rubbers on springs.'

The gang were back in the shed, laughing at Spit's account of nearly being granny-kissed to death.

'What's so funny?' he demanded. 'Have any of you ever been chased by a flirty grandma who's just discovered strawberry lip balm? No! You haven't! I think I'm going to be sick.' He thumped down on to the floor and folded his arms, looking grumpy.

'It's the weirdest hospital I've ever heard of,' said House.

'For once, you're right,' said Spit. 'I mean, hospitals are for sick people. They're places people don't like to be. So why was everyone happy?'

'I ended up playing footie,' said Alex. 'It was broken arms versus broken legs. Strangest game I've ever played.'

'Who won?' asked House.

'That's not the point, really, is it?' snapped Cherry.

'Arms,' whispered Alex, leaning across to House. 'My team!'

'Well, I got shown a knitted roast dinner,' said Inchy. 'And someone thought I was a cricket wicket and threw an orange at my head. But none of it was as weird as what Mr Kowalski told me . . .'

Everyone noticed the way his voice trailed off

suddenly. Alex stepped forward, concerned by the dark troubled look on Inchy's face.

'What did he say?'

'It's nothing,' Inchy replied. 'After all that stuff with Dante the demon geography teacher, I'm probably just overreacting.'

Alex's face was stern now. 'Tell us, Inchy.'

'He said . . . He said, "Hell is coming!".'

It was as if Inchy's words had sucked all the warmth from the shed. House shuddered. 'I don't like the sound of that.'

'"Hell is coming!",' muttered Cherry. 'Well, if it is, I bet it's got something to do with that Adonis. He's long gone off the cliff of cuckoo.'

'Cuckoo doesn't automatically equal evil crackpot,' said Spit.

'But we do know there are other demons in Green Hill,' argued Alex. 'Dante told us that much. Adonis could be one of them.'

'I agree with Spit,' said House. 'You might think we've stumbled on something all evil and dodgy, but this is nothing like what happened with Dante. This is just a hospital.'

'What about Mr Kowalski, then?' asked Cherry. 'Inchy sounds spooked by what he said.'

'I was,' Inchy replied, 'but I guess he's just one person. And he did seem a bit mad.'

'Besides,' added Spit, 'all we've got in the way of evidence to support him are some strangely happy patients, some dancing nurses with no taste in pompoms and a radio DJ who likes dressing in black. Strange? Maybe. Self-obsessed? Definitely. Evil? I don't think so.' He frowned. 'Besides, no self-respecting demon would *ever* wear that much jewellery.'

'Right,' said Alex, 'we have to admit that there's no hard proof. There could be something demonic going on, but for all we know this could be what all human hospitals are like.'

The faces around him didn't seem entirely convinced.

'Look,' Alex tried again, 'why don't we just keep an eye on things for now? We're going to be visiting every day this week, so we might as well make use of the time.'

'What, by snooping around, jumping to conclusions and getting into trouble?' said Spit. 'When we could be keeping quiet, laying low and getting back into Heaven?'

Alex turned. 'I never said anything about snooping or conclusion-jumping.'

'That only leaves –' started Cherry.

'Getting into trouble,' groaned House, shaking his head.

'*Déjà vu*,' said Spit.

5

Hate Cuisine

'You know,' said Spit, as the gang approached the hospital the following day, 'there is a reason they call it "visiting time". It's because that's when people are supposed to visit.'

'So?' replied Alex.

'So, why are we deliberately here *after* visiting time?'

'Isn't it obvious?' said Alex, coming to a halt. 'If there *is* something strange going on, it's not going to be happening when there are loads of visitors wandering around, is it? If we go during normal visiting hours, then the hospital will be just that – normal.'

'Exactly,' Spit replied, 'and then all we have to worry about is visiting a few people, eating grapes, then getting back to Tabbris and hopefully off up to Heaven. I don't know about the rest of you, but I'm pretty keen to get home.'

The rest of the team swapped shifty glances. Alex looked over at them. 'You all seem worried.'

'Not worried, exactly,' said Inchy. 'Just cautious.'

'All right,' said Alex, 'here's the deal. We go in there today and scout the place out. If we don't find anything weird –'

'What?' said Cherry. 'Like a nutter running the radio station, patients who actually want to be in hospital and nurses with pompoms?'

'OK,' Alex corrected himself, 'if we don't find anything *definitely evil*, then for the rest of the week we'll just visit at normal times, get into Tabbris's good books and get back home. Agreed?'

'But what if we do find something definitely evil?' asked House nervously. 'What then?'

'We can cross that bridge when we come to it,' said Alex quickly.

Cherry put her hands on her

as you aren't thinking of playing

again.'

Alex smiled his most innocent s.

thought hadn't crossed my mind.'

'Then why were you up until midnight last night repairing your Patented Demon Tester?' snapped Spit.

Alex's face fell. 'Fine. If you want to be boring about it, I promise not to go hunting for demons without asking Tabbris first. Happy?'

The gang nodded. Even Spit, though perhaps less enthusiastically than the others.

'So, now we can go into the hospital. Any questions?'

'Yes,' answered House. 'As it's lunchtime, does that mean I – er, I mean *we* – get to eat?'

'We'll see,' said Alex. 'Come on. We'll meet back here in an hour.'

Taking care to avoid being seen by the nurses, the gang slipped into the hospital and split up. Inchy headed back to see Mr Kowalski; Cherry and Spit set off together; and Alex and House made straight for the nearest ward.

As they pushed through the doors, the first

that greeted them was a large trolley piled high with trays, plates and steaming dishes of food.

'Ohhh!' moaned House softly, his eyes brimming.

'What's up?' asked Alex. 'You don't usually get upset at mealtimes.'

'I'm not upset, you numpty, I'm starving! And the sight of all this food just being given away . . .'

'You're having a laugh, aren't you?' exclaimed Alex. 'It's only three hours since breakfast, and you've had a snack since then.'

'That wasn't a snack, that was a "bridging sandwich". They help me get across the huge gap between meals.'

Alex shook his head, amazed at his friend's extraordinary capacity for limitless eating. But then House was substantially larger than the average angel, even for his age. He probably needed the extra fuel.

Gleefully, House practically skipped up to the trolley. But as he lifted the lid from one of the huge metal trays, his deep sigh of contentment turned into a choking gasp.

Whatever was on the menu, it was no dish

that House had ever seen before. Rather, it was an oozing and bubbling mix of sickly grey-green shades. It looked as if someone had scooped a cowpat into a frying pan and left it to boil. It seemed to move of its own accord, almost as if it were alive.

Alex felt his stomach churn. 'What *is* that?' he coughed, his hand covering his mouth and pinning his lips together as he did his best not to throw up all over the floor.

Without a word, House grabbed a plate and quickly loaded it up. Holding it at arm's length, he returned to Alex's side.

'Well?' asked Alex. 'What is it?'

'I'm not sure, but it's got pastry.'

Alex edged forward. 'That's not pastry,' he said. 'I mean, look at it — it's . . . it's *grey*!'

House peered at the menu on the trolley. 'Apparently it's chicken pie,' he said dubiously.

'Looks more like gristle cooked in snot, then covered in wet cardboard,' retorted Alex. 'This could never be called a pie.'

'Maybe not,' said House, 'but *they* seem to like it.'

He pointed at the row of patients sitting up

in their beds, enthusiastically emptying their plates. Spoons shovelled food into open mouths so fast that it seemed the patients weren't able to get the stuff inside them quickly enough. Moans of extreme happiness filled the ward after every mouthful.

House reached out a shaking hand and picked up a fork.

'You're not going to, are you?' Alex asked, as they both stared at the contents of House's plate. It wobbled slightly.

Scooping up a forkful, House closed his eyes and raised it to his lips. Then it was gone. But it didn't stay gone for long.

'PHLEURGH!'

With a roar, food sprayed from House's mouth, covering Alex from head to foot.

'Not good, then,' said Alex, wiping his eyes.

'There's no way,' spluttered House, 'that whoever made this actually *tasted* it. Or if they did, their taste buds must be totally dead.'

'Try telling that to the patients,' replied Alex. 'There is definitely something fishy going on around here. Let's find the others.'

★ ★ ★

'Ugh, this is rotten,' said Spit the moment he and Cherry entered their ward.

'True,' agreed the Cherub. 'I can't believe Alex has got us snooping around again –'

'No,' interrupted Spit, 'not that – *this*! Something's rotten in here! This room! Can't you smell it? It's like something crawled under a bed and died. And by "something" I mean an elephant.'

Cherry took a deep breath and immediately wished she hadn't.

'Ughhh!' she shrieked, her face turning as green as parts of her hair. 'What is that?'

'Whatever it is,' said Spit, waving at the rest of the room, 'why haven't *they* noticed it?'

Cherry looked. Ten patients were all happily sleeping, reading or playing cards, seemingly utterly unaware of the stink.

'They must be able to smell it!' said Cherry, her hands clamped over her nose.

'You'd think so, wouldn't you?' agreed Spit. 'But none of them seem bothered at all. It doesn't make sense. Perhaps they're here for nose operations?'

'Something weird's definitely going on,' said

Cherry, edging back to the door. 'This place smells, well, *dead*. Completely and utterly dead.'

The geriatric ward was a bustle of activity again when Inchy arrived. Three patients were holding a skidding contest on the slippery, highly polished floor, while two more were wheelchair racing around the ward. And even above all the commotion, Inchy could still hear the *clickety-click*ing of Lily's needles as she put the finishing touches on what looked like a knitted pineapple. The diminutive angel tried to sneak past the end of her bed without Lily noticing, but it didn't work.

'Inchy, my dear! It's so nice of you to pop in again! You can help me with my next project. I'm going to knit a canoe.'

'You can't knit a canoe!'

'Everyone said that about a Sunday lunch, but I proved them wrong, didn't I?' Lily gestured proudly. On top of her bedside cabinet sat her knitted roast chicken with all the trimmings. Inchy had to admit that it did look very convincing, even if Lily was clearly as mad as a hatter.

'Yes, I see,' he agreed, taking a nervous step away from the old lady. 'Well, I'd love to help, Lily, but I need to talk to Mr Kowalski.'

'Who's he, then?' asked Lily. 'A doctor?'

'No, he's another patient,' said Inchy. 'Remember? The one in the corner bed?'

'After I've done the canoe, I think I might knit a television next,' said Lily, ignoring Inchy. 'There's nothing worth watching on a real one nowadays. Well, see you later.'

Relieved to have escaped, Inchy turned to leave, but was immediately accosted by a second patient wearing a plum-coloured dressing gown that made him look like a giant bruise.

'Hello there, little man. Weren't you here yesterday? You do know it's not visiting time, don't you? You'll get into trouble if those lovely nurses find you.'

'I'm here to see Mr Kowalski,' said Inchy.

The man smiled vacantly.

'There's no one here by that name,' he said, his voice drifting slightly, as if his mind had suddenly got interested in something a long way away and gone off to see what it was. 'Perhaps you've got the wrong hospital.'

'No, I haven't,' said Inchy, a strange feeling creeping up his spine. 'I met him here yesterday. You must remember him. He's from Poland. He's . . .'

But before Inchy could finish, the old man had wandered off, almost like he'd forgotten about him completely. Fear rising, Inchy hurried down the ward to the corner bed. The curtains were tightly drawn around it.

Inchy cleared his throat. 'Mr Kowalski?'

Silence.

'Mr Kowalski, it's me, Inchy. We met yesterday.'

Still silence.

With a gulp, Inchy took hold of the curtains and swiftly pulled them open.

The corner bed was empty. But not *just* empty – it was completely bare. The sheets had been stripped to leave nothing but a fading grey mattress and a tired-looking pillow. No tablets or glasses of water stood on the bedside table, and no books or magazines were tucked into the bookcase. There was no sign of Mr Kowalski.

It was as if he'd never existed at all.

6
Just What the Doctor Ordered

'Perhaps we're being too suspicious,' said Cherry, sitting on the ground to double-check that her studs were in nice and tight. 'About the hospital, I mean.'

It was the day after their hospital investigation and the gang were getting ready for some football practice, pulling on boots, changing into shorts or, in the case of Spit, not doing anything that could be interpreted as being at all enthusiastic.

Already booted up, House was practising his skills. He flicked the ball up, caught it on his chest, volleyed it with a carefully placed knee, then hooked it left to Alex.

Or at least that's what he tried to do. Instead, he knocked the ball up, leapt for it wildly and sent it spinning high into the air, narrowly missing a startled magpie. He glanced around sheepishly, hoping no one had noticed. Everyone had, but no one said anything.

Except Spit.

'Well done. Really, I mean it. After all, if any of us had tried to do that, we would never have managed it. But to do it without even trying? That takes talent.'

'It's all right for you,' said House, looking frustrated. 'You've got used to this Earth gravity stuff. I haven't.'

'It's no different for you than it is for any of us,' replied Spit. 'Gravity is gravity.'

'But House is almost twice your size, Spit,' Alex replied, supporting his friend.

'Yeah,' said House, 'and that means I've got twice the gravity to deal with.'

Inchy opened his mouth to tell House that wasn't strictly *scientifically* true. But then he saw the look on House's face and decided against it.

Spit lapsed into a moody silence. House said nothing either but ran off to recover the ball.

Alex turned to Cherry. 'Do *you* think we're being too suspicious?'

Cherry shrugged and started to jog on the spot, warming up.

'I don't know,' she said. 'Perhaps.'

'What do you reckon, Inchy?' asked Alex.

'Well,' said Inchy, 'something has to be going on. There's no way all those patients could forget Mr Kowalski in just one day. That's impossible.'

'I hate to say it, but do you think he might be hanging out with Gabriel already?' said Cherry. 'You said he was pretty old.'

'I don't think so,' replied Inchy. 'He did have a bad cough, but he seemed really strong and fit. And besides, that doesn't explain why everyone had forgotten about him. You'd think the nurses would remember someone if they'd just died.'

'Could he have been sent home?' asked Alex. 'That's what happens when people get better.'

Inchy shook his head. 'He said he didn't want to leave his friends in danger. I can't imagine him leaving willingly.'

Spit finished tying his boots and pulled

himself up from the ground. 'Am I missing something?'

'Oh, we're just talking about the usual,' said Inchy. 'You know – hospitals, disappearing patients, the possibility of evil plots, that kind of thing.'

'There's no proof that there's an evil plot at the hospital,' said Cherry, alarmed.

'True,' said Spit, rubbing his hands together. 'But there's no proof that there isn't, is there?'

Alex looked at Spit, surprise alive in his eyes.

'You mean even *you* think something's up? Mr Sceptical, who doesn't believe in something unless it bites him on the bum?'

'Look, I may be sceptical, but I'm not stupid. We all know something about that hospital isn't right. The question is, what?'

Cherry put her hands on her hips.

'OK,' she said. 'Who are you, and what have you done with Spit?'

'Oh, ha ha,' deadpanned Spit.

'We need more information,' mused Alex. 'Whatever's going on, it could just be weird human behaviour, or it could be something worse.

We have to uncover some hard proof one way or the other.'

'The problem we've got,' said Inchy, 'is that we only ever get to go to the hospital for an hour each day, otherwise Tabbris will get suspicious. And the last thing we need is him finding out what we're up to and giving us a ten-hour lecture about how he wouldn't have been allowed to get away with our sort of behaviour when he was a trainee angel, and then never being allowed back to Heaven.'

'Yeah,' said Cherry. 'It was pretty easy to investigate Dante at school when we were there all week.'

'We need a plan,' mused Alex.

'A plan?' echoed Spit. 'Another famous Alex plan? The kind that got us into this whole stranded-on-Earth mess in the first place?'

'My plans are works of pure genius,' said Alex, sounding wounded.

'Well, can we come up with a plan *after* practice?' asked House, obviously bored with the conversation.

'Absolutely,' said Alex. 'Perhaps playing will help me think of a good idea.'

'There's a first time for everything,' muttered Spit.

Half an hour later, Alex's score was Goals: 3, Good Ideas: nil.

It was his turn in goal while the others were playing two-on-two: Cherry and House against Inchy and Spit. Inchy and Spit were two—one up, but House and Cherry weren't giving in.

Cherry had the ball.

'Man on!' bellowed House as he saw Inchy charging towards her.

Cherry caught sight of Inchy and let him get right up to her before neatly stepping left, dodging his tackle by millimetres.

Alex grinned, enjoying the battle playing out in front of him. To his left, House was waving his arms to catch Cherry's attention. Inchy had wheeled round and was now chasing after her. And Spit was right in the middle, between Cherry and the goal.

'Spit! Stop her!' yelled Inchy.

Spit raced forward.

House saw what was about to happen — Spit

was going to hold Cherry up while Inchy sneaked in from behind to steal possession!

Well, not if House had anything to do with it.

With a grunt, he pushed himself into a sprint. It wasn't graceful — when Alex ran, it was like watching an elegant cheetah; with Spit, a stealthy panther. With House, it was more like an angry hippo.

Still Cherry was oblivious to the danger. She could see Spit ahead and, beyond him, the goal. All she had to do was get past him. But unseen behind her, Inchy was gaining all the time.

And it was at that minute that Alex had a brilliant idea.

'I've got it!' shouted Alex. 'What we need is —'

But before Alex could finish, Inchy slipped round from behind Cherry and neatly stole the ball. A second later, ploughing up the ground like a tractor, House slid across the pitch and slammed into his tiny friend.

Inchy flew high into the air and turned a complete somersault before thumping back down to Earth with a sickening crunch.

'Inchy? Inchy!'

House pulled himself up from the ground as Alex, Spit and Cherry raced over to join him. They all stared down at Inchy.

'I never realized legs could bend that way,' said House.

'They can't,' replied Spit.

'Oh, Inchy,' said House, 'I'm so sorry. What have I done?'

Cherry turned to Alex. 'What were you screaming about?'

'Um, I was just going to say that what we really needed was an insider at the hospital. Someone who could pretend to be sick or injured, but who'd really be working for us, snooping about and collecting clues.'

Everyone looked down at Inchy again.

'Well,' said Spit, 'looks like there won't be any need to pretend.'

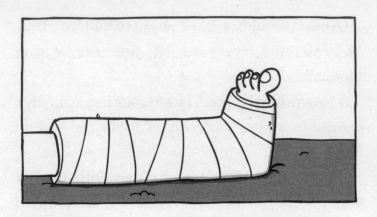

7
Laid Up

'Casualty report!' barked Tabbris as he limped into the ward, his cane tapping.

The gang looked up from their places at Inchy's bedside. The old angel's face was flinty. It certainly didn't make them feel any better. Cherry got to her feet.

'Inchy's got a broken leg, sir,' she grimaced.

'It's my fault,' said House morosely. 'I shouldn't have tackled him so hard.'

'It was an accident,' said Inchy, hoping to smooth things over. 'I had the ball. It was a fair challenge. I was just unlucky.'

'And I shouldn't have shouted,' added Alex. 'It distracted everyone at just the wrong moment.'

'Does it hurt?' asked House, staring at Inchy's enormous plaster cast, which looked almost as big as he was.

'Hurt? No,' replied Inchy sarcastically. 'Broken bones never hurt. To be honest, I think humans just break them for a laugh because it's so much fun. In fact, while you're here, shall we snap my other leg?'

Tabbris frowned. 'Is this kind of injury often sustained while playing this silly game?'

'It's very, very rare,' said Cherry desperately, seeing their footie privileges slipping away. 'Honestly. This hardly ever happens, to anyone.'

'Unless House is playing,' murmured Spit, thankfully too quietly for Tabbris to hear.

Alex gave Spit a fierce stare.

'Well,' said Tabbris with a sniff, 'it doesn't look too bad to me. I remember one mission where I crawled home with two broken arms and a torn wing. I was back on patrol within the month!' He fixed Inchy with a beady stare. 'Cod liver oil and cold baths twice a day, that's what you need. No good malingering in hospital for weeks.'

Cherry leaned over to Spit. 'It's a good job that the hospital treatments are more up to date than Tabbris's.'

'Yeah,' agreed Spit. 'If he'd been there when it happened, he'd probably have told Inchy to get up and run it off!'

Alex turned to Tabbris. 'The doctors want Inchy to stay in for at least a couple of days.'

Tabbris snorted. 'These medical chaps always think they know best. Still, I suppose we don't want to attract unwanted attention, so Inchy had better stay here for now.' He stood to his full height. 'Chin up, Inchy. I'll order in plenty of cod liver oil for when you come home.'

Inchy turned slightly green.

'The rest of you will assemble at reception in precisely five minutes.' And with that, Tabbris marched out of the ward.

Alex broke the stunned silence. 'Look,' he said, 'we haven't got much time, but we're all really sorry. We brought you these.'

House handed Inchy a brown paper bag. Inchy took it and looked inside.

'A bag of stalks?' he said, confused.

'They're grapes,' replied Cherry, snatching the bag back. She fixed House with a withering glare. 'Don't tell me you've eaten them?'

House shrugged sheepishly.

'Well they *were* grapes,' said Cherry. 'I can't believe you. First you break Inchy's leg, then you eat his grapes.'

'They were delicious, though,' said House.

'That makes me feel so much better,' huffed Inchy. 'But now that I'm here, I guess I should make myself useful, shouldn't I? It's not like I'm restricted to visiting hours any more.'

'Are you sure?' replied Alex. 'You'll have to be very careful. We still don't know what might be lurking around.'

'I survived a head-on collision with House,' sighed Inchy. 'Whatever's going on in this hospital, it can't be more dangerous than that!'

House had the good grace to look embarrassed.

'OK, then, here's the plan,' said Alex, turning to the gang conspiratorially. 'Inchy will find out what he can about what's going on in the hospital. Why everyone loves that radio show so much, why the food's so rubbish, that kind of thing. The rest of us,' he continued, 'will check up on whether Mr Kowalski might have gone home, and also investigate Aubrey Adonis. Agreed?' Everyone nodded. 'Right. Then we'd better be off. We'll meet here again tomorrow at visiting time.'

Inchy had barely had time to wave goodbye to the rest of the gang as they bundled out of the ward when the boy in the opposite bed hopped down and came over to him.

'Hi,' he said. 'I'm Jim. You're Inchy, aren't you?'

Inchy nodded.

'I heard your friends call you that. Doesn't seem very fair to be called that just because you're small.'

Inchy smiled. 'Doesn't bother me,' he said. 'My brain's bigger than all of theirs put together!'

Jim laughed and sat down on a chair at the side of Inchy's bed.

'What are you in for?' asked Inchy.

'Armed robbery,' said Jim.

Inchy looked startled.

'Only joking!' sniggered Jim. 'It's ingrowing toenails. Not very fancy, really. Doesn't impress the girls or anything. What about you?'

Inchy pulled back his sheet.

'Wow! That's awesome!' said Jim, staring wide-eyed at the huge cast on Inchy's leg.

'No, it's not, it's painful,' winced Inchy.

'How did you do it?'

'House fell on me.'

Jim's jaw dropped. 'A house fell on you? What happened? How did you get out? Did you have to be rescued?'

Inchy smiled. 'Actually, it was a footie accident,' he said. 'My friend came in too hard with a tackle. His name's Big House — he was the one who was just here.'

Jim caught the football reference. 'Who do you support?'

'Pardon?'

'Which team? I'm a Man U fan.'

Inchy opened his mouth, but before he could speak the other boy dashed back to his own bed, returning a moment later with a large album filled with stickers.

'Check this out,' he said, flicking through pages

of players all standing proud. 'I've nearly collected the lot. Cool or what?'

Inchy gazed down into a sea of faces. He'd seen a few on television now and again, but he certainly couldn't put names to any of them. Except one.

'Is that Beckham?'

'Yeah,' said Jim. 'All the ones on this page have been captains. Becks doesn't play for us any more, though. He's amazing, isn't he?'

As Jim continued to sing Beckham's praises, Inchy did his best to nod in all the right places, as if he knew what Jim was talking about. This was one of the problems with being an angel on Earth – he didn't know that much about Earth football teams, but he couldn't really explain that to Jim.

Inchy suddenly realized that Jim had stopped talking and was looking at him expectantly.

'Pardon?'

'I said, "Have you listened to *Brain Dead* yet?"'

'*Brain Dead*?' said Inchy, pretending he didn't know about it. 'What's that?'

'It's a show on the hospital radio. Aubrey Adonis

is the host. You're going to love it!' said Jim. 'It's awesome! Like medicine or something. When I got here, my feet were killing me. They put me on painkillers and stuff, but listening to *Brain Dead* seems to make everything so much better. Does that sound weird?'

'I guess not,' said Inchy, wary at the mention of the creepy DJ. 'Music always makes me feel better about stuff.'

'Yeah, that's what it's like,' said Jim. 'Adonis is amazing!'

As if on cue, a nurse burst into the ward. She did a quick rustle-tussle with her pompoms, then lifted up a huge board with the words *Brain Dead in Five Minutes!* printed on it.

'Remember, everyone,' she said, smiling broadly, 'tune into the fun and tune out of the pain!'

Inchy expected the nurse to disappear again, but instead she came over to his bed.

'And I've got a special announcement for you, you lucky little boy!' The nurse's eyes gleamed manically as she turned to the rest of the ward so they could all hear. 'Aubrey Adonis is coming to pay you a special visit – because he loves to welcome his new listeners in person!'

'Wow!' said Jim. 'A visit from Adonis! How lucky are we?'

'Er . . . I don't know,' said Inchy. 'Very?'

'You bet!' said Jim, standing up. 'Adonis is so cool. And he's visiting you!'

At that very moment, the doors to the ward were flung open and in strode Adonis, flanked by another pair of cheerleader nurses. The ward went nuts. An old man in the corner whooped so loudly his teeth fell out. A younger man with long hair and rather too many tattoos spun on his crutches.

Adonis waved lazily before perching on the side of Inchy's bed. Then he reached up and removed his silver-rimmed, mirror-lensed sunglasses.

'So, Inchy, how are you?'

Inchy didn't know if he was imagining things, but it sounded almost as though Adonis was on the edge of tears. He stared at the huge man sitting next to him. Around his neck hung so many gold chains it was like his head sat on top of a metal altar. His fingers were barely visible beneath dozens of rings. Inchy opened his mouth to speak, but no words came to his rescue.

'I know, I know,' said Adonis, placing a heavy hand on Inchy's shoulder. 'Being in hospital isn't easy. It's so very hard. But . . .' Adonis paused, almost as if he was trying to build up the tension in the ward, '. . . it's like a caterpillar becoming a butterfly. It has a long struggle to get free from its cocoon, but when it does, it becomes so beautiful.'

Inchy obviously looked confused because Adonis turned back to him and said, 'It's through such pain as yours that something beautiful can be born, Inchy.'

Inchy didn't have the faintest idea what Adonis was talking about. There was nothing beautiful about this hospital.

Adonis spoke again. 'Anyway, I'm here to help,' he said, squeezing Inchy's shoulder. 'It's my role in this life to bring comfort to people. I only wish I could do it better.'

'Er, I want to help people too,' chirped Jim suddenly.

'You know,' said Adonis, gazing across to Jim,

'that is the most heart-warming thing I've heard all day. You are a brave young man, Jim. Ever so brave.'

'Thank you!' said Jim, almost shaking with excitement.

'And you know,' said Adonis, 'I can see you helping people. Lots of people. In fact, I can see you helping me with something very important. Would you like that?'

Jim's face was a picture of star-struck excitement. 'Yes!' he cried. 'Anything!'

'Thank you,' whispered Adonis, staring at Jim with wide eyes. 'You'll be perfect.'

'So what do you want me to do?'

'Don't you worry about that at the moment,' said Adonis. 'Rest now and I'll tell you when the time comes.'

Jim tucked himself into bed, obviously keen to get the resting out of the way as quickly as possible.

'Here,' said Adonis, handing Inchy a little silk bag. 'I'd like you to have these.'

Inchy opened the bag to find a pair of *Brain Dead* earphones.

'I, er, thanks –' started Inchy, but Adonis was

already at the door. He paused, then flashed the ward a peace sign.

'My friends . . . Enjoy the show!'

And with that, he was gone.

'He's just so amazing, don't you think?' said Jim with a sigh. 'You'd better plug those headphones in – the show starts any second!'

Inchy didn't know what to think. Jim had seemed pretty normal at first, but now he sounded like he'd be willing to run over hot coals for the hospital DJ. Surely that was a bit odd?

As for Adonis himself . . . well, he certainly looked strange, but he had sounded sincere about wanting to help people. Hadn't they been taught at Cloud Nine Academy that it was wrong to judge someone on their appearance? What if the gang was wrong about Adonis?

Inchy shook his head. There was too much to think about. For now, the best he could do was to listen to *Brain Dead* and see what all the fuss was about. He plugged in his earphones. It was only a radio show, after all; what possible harm could it do?

All at once, music filled his head. It was lovely – peaceful and relaxing, like a nice warm bed.

Suddenly, Inchy's eyelids felt heavy, like thick gold chains were attached to his eyelashes, weighing them down. The last thing he heard was a strangely familiar voice crooning softly into his ear, whispering soothing words. Then gentle darkness took him and Inchy slipped into a dreamless sleep.

8
Mission Impractical

The morning after Inchy's accident, the gang assembled to work out their next move. There was a mood of quiet determination around the breakfast table. House was even paying more attention to Alex than to the contents of his plate.

'Right, here's the plan –' began Alex.

But before he could finish, Alex was interrupted by the appearance of Tabbris in the kitchen doorway.

'What's going on here? Is something wrong with my porridge?' asked Tabbris, noticing the still-full bowls that had been pushed aside. 'Ah! Not enough salt, that'll be it. You should've said! I'll put another spoonful in tomorrow.'

'Oh no, it's not that,' said Cherry hurriedly. 'We're just not very hungry.'

'Nonsense,' sniffed Tabbris. 'Breakfast is the most important meal of the day. Don't forget that an army marches on its stomach – I remember having to tell old Napoleon the same thing. Why don't you have some toast instead?'

Smiling her most innocent smile, Cherry plucked a piece of cold toast from the wire rack in the middle of the table. The gang knew from experience that the quicker they did as they were told, the sooner Tabbris would go away.

But this time, Tabbris didn't go away. He stood bolt upright at the head of the table.

'I want to talk to you seriously,' he announced.

The gang held their breath. Did Tabbris know they'd been snooping around the hospital outside visiting hours?

'I've been keeping a close eye on you over the past few days,' said Tabbris, 'and I think you should all know . . . I'm very impressed with your behaviour.'

'Pardon?'

Alex couldn't believe his ears! Was it possible that the old angel hadn't rumbled them, after all?

'You *seem* to be making progress,' continued Tabbris doubtfully, almost as if he couldn't quite believe it himself. 'You're taking your community service seriously and working together as a unit. This can't be ignored.' Tabbris paused. 'I'm pleased to tell you that I will be sending a good report back to Gabriel this week.'

No one in the gang knew what to say. Having expected a telling-off, they were doubly stunned by this sudden good news.

Finally, Alex stepped in. 'Thank you, sir. We are trying our hardest to be good.'

'We really are,' added Cherry in support. 'We want to get back to Heaven as soon as possible so we can become real angels.'

'Quite right too,' said Tabbris, crossing to the door. 'But there's no room for slacking now. Carry on!'

As soon as he was gone, the gang let out a collective sigh of relief.

'I was sure he was on to us,' said Cherry.

'Me too,' moaned House. 'I was so nervous my knees were practically knocking.'

'But he's not,' beamed Alex. 'He doesn't have a clue. So Operation Adonis can proceed as planned!'

'Hold on,' said Spit. 'Tabbris may not know what we're up to, but what he just said changes things, doesn't it? I mean, if he sends a good report to Gabriel, we could be back home by next week. We don't want to mess that up.'

'We won't be messing it up!' said Alex. 'We'd be doing what we're supposed to do as angels — protecting humans from demonic activity.'

'But we still don't know for sure that there is any demonic activity at the hospital,' replied Cherry. 'And it's not our job to protect humans yet — we're not qualified angels. And I want to go home. Now. Sooner if possible. I miss the Academy and our other friends. And I miss having my wings — I even miss lessons.'

'And I miss those wonderful syrup sponge puddings they serve on Sundays,' sighed House. 'So light and fluffy!'

Spit nodded. 'I mean, what exactly do you expect to find, Alex? Is it really worth risking the best chance we've had of getting home?'

'Well, we won't know that until we find out what we're dealing with, will we?' said Alex frustratedly.

'But imagine if there turns out to be nothing demonic at the hospital and we get caught snooping around,' protested Spit. 'There's no way we'll ever get back to Heaven then. Tabbris will have us on double chores forever!'

'And that would be rubbish,' finished Cherry.

'I know!' hissed Alex. 'But we can't sit by and do nothing. We got into trouble for fighting Dante, but if we hadn't done it, then that demon egg would have hatched and Green Hill would have been overrun by evil demons.'

'Exactly,' agreed House loyally. 'Imagine if we don't do anything now and then something like that happens at the hospital. It would be awful.'

A heavy silence hung over the table as everyone imagined what might happen if their worst fears were realized. Finally, Spit sighed.

'Well, at least Inchy will have some company if we all get beaten up by demons.'

Cherry gave Spit a look. 'And I guess there's no *real* harm in doing a bit of investigating,' she shrugged. 'So I'll try to find out if Mr Kowalski has really disappeared or whether he's sitting happily at home in front of the telly.'

'I'll come with you,' said House protectively.

'I can look after myself,' Cherry shot back. 'Just because I'm a girl, it doesn't mean I'm weak and feeble.'

House's face fell. He wondered whether, after the accident with Inchy, the gang would ever trust him again. Luckily, Cherry saw his doleful expression and relented.

'Actually, House,' she said, 'let's stick together. Two heads are better than one.'

House smiled at her and mouthed a *Thanks*.

'That means you're with me, then,' said Alex to Spit.

'Hurrah,' said Spit. 'Oh, the joy.'

'And,' continued Alex, ignoring Spit's sarcasm, 'I reckon we should try to find out everything we can about Adonis.'

'And how do we do that?'

'Well,' said Alex, 'I'm guessing that when Adonis joined the hospital radio, it was reported in the local paper. He's not exactly publicity-shy, is he? So why don't we check out the newspaper archives and see what we can uncover?'

'Right,' said Cherry, standing up. 'Let's get going. We'll all meet back at the shed at lunchtime.'

'Oi! Who made you leader?' asked Alex rather crossly.

'Well, somebody's got to take charge or we'd be sitting here talking all day!' said Cherry, twirling an arrow between her fingers. 'Come on, House, let's go!'

Inchy's mind was a swirling whirlpool. He felt almost like he had his wings back and was flying again, soaring around inside a tornado of spinning colours and sounds. He couldn't tell how long he was immersed in the kaleidoscope of shifting lights, but finally the colours slowly faded and he woke up.

For a moment, blinking in the sunlight, Inchy couldn't work out where he was. Then he remembered. The tackle by House that had gone just a little bit wrong. The journey to the hospital. The cast being put on his broken leg. Tabbris and the rest of the gang sitting by his bedside. Aubrey Adonis stopping by to give him some earphones. Tuning in to *Brain Dead*. Then . . . Then . . .

Inchy frowned. He supposed he must have fallen asleep, but he had no memory of drifting off. No dreams. Nothing. A complete blank. It was like he'd slipped on the earphones and passed out.

Before Inchy could think about it any more, though, a nurse appeared. Like all the others, she was extremely pretty, with sparkling blue eyes and platinum blonde hair done in an elaborate style. Although she was wheeling a large trolley down the ward, she seemed so glamorous she wouldn't have looked out of place on the red carpet at the Oscars.

'Good morning, Inchy!' she trilled, handing him a steaming bowl. 'Time for breakfast!'

The idea of breakfast struck Inchy as a very good idea indeed. He vaguely remembered something Big House had said about the hospital food not being very good, but he couldn't recall exactly what it was. It probably wasn't important. Anyway, he thought, as he peered into his bowl, House must have been talking about somewhere else entirely – this food looked delicious.

Filled with hunger and enthusiasm, Inchy grabbed his spoon and took a large mouthful. It was exquisite. Nothing like the salty mush that Tabbris served up each morning under the misleading name of porridge.

As Inchy sank back against his pillows with a contented sigh, he realized that, despite a slight throbbing in his broken leg, he felt very happy indeed. Hospital wasn't so bad, after all. It was fine. In fact, it was better than fine, it was *great*! His bed was comfy and warm, the food was delicious, and everyone around him – from the patients and the nurses to the titan of cool that was Aubrey Adonis – were all such lovely people.

Taking another mouthful, he glanced over at the bed opposite. It looked like all the other beds in the ward: white, clean and comfortable. But there was one significant difference – it was empty.

Inchy was pretty sure there had been somebody in that bed yesterday, but he just couldn't remember the name. Jack? No, that wasn't right. Jake? No . . . Jim! That was it – Jim! The bed had been Jim's, hadn't it?

'Nurse!' he called. 'Nurse!'

Almost at the speed of light, a radiant nurse appeared at Inchy's bedside.

'Yes, dear?'

'Where's Jim?'

'Who's Jim?' replied the nurse with a smile.

'He was in that bed over there.'

The nurse looked across the ward, then back to Inchy.

'Oh, he's been discharged,' she said.

Inchy felt strangely satisfied with the answer. Jim must've got better and been sent home. Of course. Still . . .

'I didn't hear him leave.'

'Well, you must've been asleep,' said the nurse sympathetically. 'Now eat your porridge, there's a good boy.'

'And he didn't say goodbye,' said Inchy sadly.

'Never mind, dear,' soothed the nurse. '*Brain Dead* will be on soon and that will take your mind off things. Don't forget to tune in – it'll make you feel so much better!'

Inchy smiled at the thought of *Brain Dead*. He was already really looking forward to it. With a final warming smile, the nurse smoothed down Inchy's crisp white bedsheet and skipped away down the ward.

Turning back to his breakfast, Inchy felt very glad that it wasn't *him* who'd been sent home. Indeed, he couldn't even imagine leaving the hospital. He had a faint recollection that he was supposed to be *doing* something while he was here, but he couldn't remember what. And surely it couldn't matter. After all, what could possibly be more important than *Brain Dead*? Yes, hospital was just great and Inchy knew he wanted to stay forever.

Lifting another spoonful of creamy porridge to his lips, Inchy's eyes slid carelessly across the empty bed opposite him. As they did, he noticed that just sticking out from under the mattress was the corner of a glossy cover. Like a magazine or a sticker album.

A sticker album!

Inchy felt as if he'd been drenched with a

bucket of ice-cold water. The comfortable feelings he'd been enjoying vanished like a puff of smoke. Jim was so proud of his sticker album, there was no way he'd ever leave it behind. Something was wrong. And suddenly Inchy remembered all the other strange things about the hospital – the cheesy nurses and the horrible food. He glanced down into his spoon.

Yeuch! The porridge he had just been about to scoff down was a dirty grey colour, flecked with green. It looked like sick. Inchy felt his stomach turn at the thought of how much of it he'd already eaten. How could he ever have thought it was nice? With a jolt of horror, Inchy realized the truth.

Brain Dead. Ever since he had listened to Adonis's show, Inchy had started to become just like the other patients – strangely happy to be in the hospital, and perfectly content to eat the horrible food.

'Mr Kowalski was right,' muttered Inchy to himself. 'There's something very wrong here.'

Inchy shook his head. He'd been under the influence of *Brain Dead* too, but now he was free and could think clearly. First Mr Kowalski had disappeared, now Jim. And wherever they had gone, it certainly wasn't home. Setting his jaw grimly, Inchy made a decision. Someone had to find them.

And that someone was him.

9
Looking for Answers

'Right,' said House, marching purposefully ahead of Cherry, 'we're going to do this by the book. No mistakes. No tripping up. No way anyone gets hurt. Understood?'

Cherry skipped up behind, grinning.

'Yes, Master Chief!'

'Yeah,' House growled, pulling a piece of paper from his pocket. 'By the book. I copied this down just before we left. It's from my Guardian Angel textbook. If we follow these guidelines, nothing goes wrong.'

Cherry scanned the words scrawled on to the

page. House's handwriting was just like the rest of him – big enough to be easily seen from a distance.

'So this guide of yours suggests we do a door-to-door search, yeah?'

House nodded, a proud smile splashing across his face.

'Which means knocking on every door in Green Hill and asking if Mr Kowalski is in?'

House nodded again, although his smile had faded slightly.

'So how long do you think that'll take?'

'Eh?'

'How long? I mean, there are about a thousand houses in Green Hill, and just you and me to search them. Oh, and we can't fly, so we'll be doing it all on foot. And we're not fully qualified yet, so we can't even do time-slipping.'

'Time-slipping?' asked House.

'Don't you remember? We'll learn about it when we get to Level Three – how angels can zoom all over the place, be in two places at once and do loads of stuff really, really quickly. It's pretty cool.'

'But we can't do that now?'

'House, we can't even fly in this place. We need another plan. And this is it.' Cherry pointed across the road.

'Your plan is to buy one Burger Shack burger and get another one free?' asked House, staring at a huge poster on the far side of the street. 'I'm up for that, but I don't see how it'll help us find Mr Kowalski. Unless he's at Burger Shack too.'

'No!' said Cherry, resisting the urge to whack House over the head. 'Next to the poster – the phone box!'

'I don't think people live in phone boxes,' said House solemnly. 'In fact, I know they don't.'

Cherry opened her mouth to say something, but thought better of it. Instead, she grabbed House by his sleeve and hauled him over the road like a parent dragging a small child away from something dangerous.

'You're quite rough for a girl,' said House as Cherry pushed him into the phone box. 'Aren't Cherubs supposed to be gentle and happy and fun-loving?'

'You're thinking of puppies,' said Cherry. 'Now look –' she picked up a thick book hanging from a rope next to the phone – 'I'm going to use this. It's a phone book and it has the numbers of everyone who lives in Green Hill.'

House watched as Cherry flicked through the pages. She had some difficulty doing so. Inside a phone box, House didn't leave much room for anything else.

'Ah!'

'Ah?'

'Look!' House glanced down to see what Cherry was pointing at. 'See? Only one Kowalski! How easy was that? It would've taken ages to find the right address going door-to-door.'

'Do you ever get tired of being right?' asked House.

'Nope,' smirked Cherry. 'Let's go!'

'Do you know what I don't like about this plan?' asked Spit, turning to Alex.

The pair had just left number 92 Eccles Road and were now on their way to the newspaper archives.

'No,' replied Alex. 'What?'

'Everything.'

'So, do you have a better idea?'

'Even if I did, it wouldn't make any difference,' grumbled Spit. 'It's only your plans that we ever end up trying.'

Alex stopped. 'Right, out with it. What's really bugging you?'

Spit turned and scowled. 'I just want to get back to Heaven,' he said.

'You don't think I want to stay here, do you?' asked Alex.

'Sometimes I wonder,' said Spit, shoving his hands deep into his pockets. 'I mean, your plans have a habit of backfiring.'

'This one won't,' argued Alex.

'You don't know that for sure,' said Spit. 'We thought we'd done well last time, defeating Dante and everything, but it still got us into trouble. And I don't want to get into trouble again. I just want to go home!'

'Look,' said Alex in exasperation, 'I want to get back too. And I know Cherry's right about us not being demon hunters, but there's something suspicious about that hospital. And it's not like we're doing anything bad in trying to find out what it is. That's not against the rules. It's not like with Mr Dante when we *knew* he was a demon and didn't tell anyone. We don't know who or what Adonis is. That's what we need to discover.'

Spit gave a grudging nod. 'So what makes you think we'll find anything useful in these old newspapers, then?'

'Adonis's ego,' said Alex. 'It's huge. He loves to talk about himself so much that he's bound to have let something slip. If he has, we might find hard proof that he's up to no good.'

'You sound like you actually want Adonis to be evil,' replied Spit. 'Wouldn't it be better if we found out that he was just normal? You know, a human, but with a screw loose?'

Alex turned to Spit. 'Ye-es,' he admitted with a smirk, 'but it wouldn't be as much fun . . .'

Pulling on his dressing gown, Inchy hauled himself upright on a small pair of crutches. Looking right and left to make sure there were no nurses in view, he scuttled over to the door of the ward.

In the corridor, he paused. Where to begin? Inchy racked his brains for any trace of a clue as to where Mr Kowalski and Jim could have disappeared to, but no answers came.

'In that case,' murmured the diminutive angel, 'I'll just start by looking around.'

For the next two hours, Inchy roamed the corridors looking for leads. Everything seemed normal. Every ward, every floor, every staircase. The waiting rooms were quiet, the reception efficient and busy, the lifts happily whizzing people up and down between levels. There was nothing out of the ordinary at all.

Inchy limped from ward to ward until he was thoroughly hot and bothered and his arms ached with the effort of dragging himself around on his crutches. In each one the patients were happy and calm. Some were playing cards with each other, others were chatting to the nurses and *everyone* was talking about *Brain Dead*.

It all came back to *Brain Dead*. It was clear that the radio show was somehow responsible for keeping the patients in their unnatural state of happiness and contentment. That meant that Adonis had to be behind it. But behind *what*? *Why* was he doing it?

Inchy growled with frustration. The gang were depending on him for inside information, but he'd discovered almost nothing. The hospital's dirty secrets were eluding him . . . and that was when he noticed it.

Dirt.

It wasn't much, but it was there – and it was in the strangest of places: mud under the otherwise immaculate fingernails of a nurse, a smudge of grime on a pure white bedsheet, and, right next to Inchy, a single grubby footprint on the floor.

Inchy had just turned towards it to have a closer look when a middle-aged lady patient strolled by, happily listening to an iPod. It was only when she'd passed that Inchy noticed the remains of a thistle tangled into her bright orange hair.

Inchy reached up to rub his eyes. Nothing was making any sense. Hospitals were supposed to be clean places, weren't they? So where was the dirt coming from? Before Inchy could work out a plausible explanation, though, something caught his eye that almost made him gasp aloud.

Because as he lowered his fingers, he noticed that his own fingernails were clogged with mud. And he had no idea how it had got there. No idea at all.

10
Danger Signs

'Call me old-fashioned,' said Cherry, 'but I think that people usually only answer the door after someone knocks.'

House turned to her, his hand hovering in mid-air in front of the door – as it had been for the past two minutes.

'I'm *about* to knock,' he said. 'I'm just working out what I'm going to say when whoever lives here answers, that's all.'

Cherry sighed. 'They won't be expecting a witty speech, you twonk,' she said. 'Just say who you are and ask if Mr Kowalski is in.'

'Right.' House turned back to the door. Then a second later he turned back to Cherry again. 'Why am *I* doing this?'

'Because you said it was your job,' Cherry replied. 'You said how if anything was going to happen then you'd rather it happened to you first. It was all very brave and heroic.'

'Oh yeah,' said House with a not-very-convincing smile.

'Well?' said Cherry.

House turned back to the big red door. Without giving himself time to think, he rapped his fist once against the painted wood and immediately turned to go.

'That's it, no one home.'

Cherry glared at him. 'Let's give them more than a microsecond to get to the door, shall we?'

'Absolutely,' said House. 'I was just, well, you know –'

'Yes? Can I help?' a voice interrupted.

Standing in the doorway was an old lady. She looked like the kind of person a company would use to advertise comfortable chairs. She gave the two angels a big warm smile, and her eyes seemed to twinkle with years of experience and wisdom.

'Er, hi,' spluttered House. 'I, er, well, we . . .'

Grinning, Cherry came to the rescue. House got flustered so easily that it almost took all the fun out of watching him. Almost.

'Hello. I'm Cherry and this is my friend House. We're doing a school project on the history of the town and wondered if —'

'Would you like to come in for some tea and cake?' the old lady interrupted. 'Two young people like you need plenty of food to keep you going, I'd say.'

House's face lit up and he miraculously found his voice again. 'All right! Come on, Cherry!'

As House took a step through the door, Cherry grabbed his arm. 'What happened to being careful?' she hissed.

House turned and looked at her with an incredulous smile on his face. 'Are you serious? She looks about a hundred and seventy! Besides, she has cake.'

Cherry unleashed a glare that could have skewered an elephant. Then turned to the old lady, all sweetness. 'We just came to ask you some questions, that's all,' she said.

'Well, questions can be very tiring,' said the

old lady, 'so why don't we do the questions over cake?'

'That would be lovely,' said Cherry as politely as she could, acutely aware that, next to her, House was practically drooling.

'Take a seat. I'll only be two minutes,' said the lady as House and Cherry edged through the door to find themselves in a small cosy living room. They sat down on a tired but comfortable sofa as their host disappeared into the kitchen.

'Cake!' said House, unconsciously licking his lips.

'Will you stop that!' whispered Cherry fiercely. 'We're here on serious business!'

'I know,' House whispered back. 'Cake is a very serious business indeed.'

Cherry was just about to say something extremely rude when the old lady reappeared.

'Here you go, my dears,' she said, setting down a large tray containing the world's biggest teapot, three chipped mugs and a five-tier stand groaning under the weight of every sort of cake that even House could possibly have imagined. The display defied all the laws of gravity and healthy eating at the same time – it was like staring into a black hole made entirely of sugar and cream.

The old lady sat down. 'I'm afraid I've forgotten your names,' she said with a smile.

'House and Cherry,' smiled Cherry. 'We go to Green Hill School.'

'Oh yes, that was it! And I'm Vera Kowalski. Cake?'

House didn't need to be asked twice. Five seconds later, he was tucking into a large piece of chocolate gateau, with three doughnuts, some fruit loaf, a slice of Victoria sponge and a thick piece of tiffin stacked on his plate in reserve.

'Nice?' asked Vera.

'Mmmph!' replied House. 'Luffly! Deliffous!'

Cherry stared at him and whispered, 'Remember, we're here for more than just the cake, OK?'

'Oh absolutely,' said House, swallowing. 'Could you pass me one of those scones?'

Shaking her head, Cherry reached out, took a single doughnut and sat back in her chair. 'Thank you for seeing us,' she said to Vera. 'We were told at school that Mr Kowalski was very good at telling old stories about Green Hill, but no one mentioned all the lovely treats!'

Vera smiled. 'Oh yes, my husband can spin a few yarns, though he does tend to go on a bit.'

'Could we possibly talk to him?'

'I'm afraid not,' said Vera. 'He's at the hospital. He went in two weeks ago. His knees and elbows were playing up. But then he will insist on doing all that silly keep-fit stuff!'

Even through House's overflowing mouthful of cake, Cherry could see his mind was also racing. Mr Kowalski wasn't at home. Something must have happened to him. And whatever that something was, it must have happened at the hospital.

With a sinking feeling, Cherry wondered how long it would be before Inchy's investigations uncovered more than he bargained for. She and House had to get to the hospital double quick. But first they would have to go back to Eccles Road.

Cherry wasn't about to set foot in that hospital again without her bow.

'This is pointless,' said Spit. 'There's nothing here.'

'Come on,' replied Alex. 'The archivist told us

that Adonis arrived some time last year. We've only got one more month to check.'

Spit huffed. The pair had spent at least an hour flicking through the pages of old newspapers, looking for a trace of information about Adonis. So far, they'd found nothing, although Alex had become strangely absorbed by weird and wonderful news stories. The one about a man arrested during a robbery who claimed to be his own long-lost twin brother made him chuckle. As did the story about the cow that thought it was a duck – right up until it tried to jump into a pond and discovered it couldn't swim. Just as he found himself being sucked into an item about a woman who'd invented a new way to grow rhubarb, Spit's voice cut in.

'Oh my word! I've got something!'

Alex turned to look. 'What is it?'

'See for yourself.'

Alex took the paper. Staring up from the front page was a huge picture of Adonis in a radio studio. He was all gleaming smile and puppy-dog eyes.

'It's from when he joined the hospital as resident DJ,' added Spit. 'His first interview.'

Alex read the story. To his annoyance it said very little. Adonis just waffled on for ages about how blessed he felt to be given an opportunity to use his talents to help heal people who were really in need.

'Do you think he ever says anything that isn't really, really cheesy?' muttered Alex.

Spit shook his head.

'So what got you so excited?' Alex asked, confused.

'Look at the picture,' said Spit tensely.

Alex did exactly that. He looked really, really close. Close enough to see the spot on Adonis's nose and the half-eaten sandwich on a plate near a microphone. But that was all he could see. Alex turned back to Spit with a shrug.

'I don't see it.'

'The shelf behind Adonis,' said Spit. 'Just above his left ear.'

Alex squinted again. For a moment, all he could see was a smudgy blur. Then the shape resolved itself into a large black book, and a dagger of ice cut into Alex's heart.

'It can't be.'

'It is.'

'But it can't be. We buried it, remember? We buried it!'

'Well,' said Spit, 'I'm guessing that the one we've got isn't the only copy.'

'It's . . . It's –'

'It's the *Necronomicon*,' finished Spit. '*The Book of the Dead*. The manual for evil-doers everywhere. It's there, on Adonis's shelf, at the hospital.'

'With Inchy.'

'Exactly,' replied Spit. 'With Inchy.'

For a long moment, Inchy stared at his dirty fingernails. How had they *got* dirty? He'd only just woken up! It didn't make any sense at all. Fingernails didn't just get dirty overnight.

'Right,' muttered Inchy. 'I want answers. And the only person who's likely to have them is Aubrey Adonis. And the best place to find him will be the radio studio.'

With that, Inchy set off, his crutches *tap-tapping* on the hard corridor tiles. Catching a lift up to the third floor, he had no trouble in locating the studio. Arrows pointed the way, each one decorated with life-size pictures of Adonis. On one wall, someone had painted a huge mural showing the DJ rising over a green hill like a dark sun, one hand cupped against the side of his head. Above the picture, a huge sign read, *If you need an ear, Adonis is here!*

Finally, Inchy rounded a corner and found himself outside a big door. It reminded him uncomfortably of the door to Gabriel's office back at Cloud Nine Academy. Only this door was painted entirely black. It looked like someone had carved a hole into outer space.

Allowing curiosity to take over, Inchy moved closer. He raised his hand, preparing to knock, then stopped. He could hear a voice. It was ever so faint, and muffled by the heavy door, but it was somehow familiar. Adonis?

It certainly sounded a bit like Adonis, but something was different. When he'd visited Inchy in the ward, Adonis's voice had been a cheesy mixture of sincerity and care, laced with a dash of helplessness, like a bad talkshow host. But the voice he could now hear was something else entirely. It was cold and harsh, like ice falling on to a metal floor. Inchy pressed his ear up against the door.

'I give you my word, master,' said Adonis, his

new voice sending waves of fear through Inchy. 'One more day and you will have all the soldiers that you need.'

With a gasp, Inchy jumped away from the door as if it was red hot. Whatever Adonis was up to, it obviously wasn't about taking away people's pain. And suddenly, knocking on the door didn't seem like such a good idea any more.

Backing off, Inchy turned to go, only to find his way blocked.

'Well, Inchy, my dear, what are we doing out of bed?'

Inchy recognized the nurse as one from his own ward. Her bright shiny teeth grinned down at him like a great white shark's.

'Er, um . . . I was just coming to see Mr Adonis,' he lied. 'But he's not in.'

The nurse leaned towards him, flickering her eyelashes, and for a horrible moment Inchy thought that she was going to knock on the door and check. Instead, she placed her hand on his forehead.

'How are you feeling?'

'I'm fine,' said Inchy nervously, 'just fine.'

The nurse leaned in even closer. Inchy could

smell her breath. It was sweet, sickly sweet, like honey. He suddenly remembered what Mr Kowalski had said about the nurses being involved with the mystery of the hospital, and how they suspected him. Did this one suspect Inchy? Was he about to disappear, just like Mr Kowalski?

'Well,' she said, 'even so, you shouldn't leave the ward without permission. You might get into all kinds of trouble! Back to bed for you.'

Inchy breathed a sigh of relief as the nurse took a gentle hold of him and led him away from the studio. But that relief disappeared as they re-entered the ward and the nurse's grip on his arm grew suddenly tighter.

'Now, into bed we go.'

Lifting Inchy off his feet, the nurse whipped back the covers and deposited him into the bed.

'Now, you stay here,' she continued, tucking the sheets so tight around him that his arms were pinned to his sides. 'You just have to let us care for you. That's all we ask. All Adonis asks. It's not much, you know! And it's for your own good. There now!'

The nurse sighed as she stood back to admire

her handiwork. Inchy was practically strapped to the bed. He could only watch as she leaned over to place a set of headphones on his ears. She did it gently, as if she was afraid she was doing something that might hurt him. Then she kissed him on the forehead.

'It's time for *Brain Dead* now, Inchy, so why don't you just lie back, close your eyes and let Adonis guide you along the road to recovery?'

As the nurse turned and glided away, Inchy could feel his heart thrashing in his chest like a caged bird. *Brain Dead* was about to start! The thought filled him with dread. Inchy just knew that if he listened to the programme again, he would forget everything he had discovered.

The nurse was back at her desk now, her own headphones in place, just like all the other patients in the ward. Desperately, Inchy wriggled his body, trying to slip free from the snakelike hug of the sheets.

It worked! One arm came slightly loose. Fumbling about, Inchy's scrabbling fingers found the headphones' lead, grasped it firmly and –

'Welcome to *Brain Dead*!'

Adonis's voice filled Inchy's head, swelling like

an orchestra. His fingers relaxed and he felt his head fall back on to his soft, soft pillow as soothing music caressed his ears. It was so relaxing, so calming. It would be easy just to let go. Inchy felt the pain in his leg begin to slip away . . .

No! The team were counting on him. He couldn't let them down.

Summoning up his last reserves of concentration, Inchy seized the lead and pulled the headphones from their socket.

Silence.

Panting, Inchy opened his eyes. The nurse didn't seem to have noticed anything. She was still sitting at her desk, earphones on, eyes glazed. The other patients looked the same – blissfully happy and utterly unaware of the world around them.

Shaking his head, Inchy untangled the rest of his body from the bedsheets. It was time to find out what was going on. And now that everyone was in *Brain Dead* mode, there shouldn't be anyone moving around the hospital to stop him.

Hopping out of bed on to his crutches, Inchy edged to the door. He was just about to slip out when something made him stop. It was a prickling sensation on the back of his neck.

Fear.

It was still quite a new emotion for Inchy. Back at Cloud Nine, the only thing that went bump in the night was House falling down the stairs as he tried to sneak into the kitchen for a midnight feast. But Inchy was scared now as he looked back at the ward.

For a moment, there was utter stillness. The patients sat unmoving, their eyes glassed over.

Then, in perfect unison, everyone in the room turned their heads towards him.

11

Brain Dead

Inchy stared in horror. The patients' eyes were glazed and distant. Their faces were impassive masks, their mouths open, tongues hanging out, drool spilling to the floor in slow gloopy drips.

As he watched, they removed their headphones and started to get out of bed, their movements jerky and uncoordinated. Whatever *Brain Dead* was, and whatever Adonis was doing with it, listening to the programme had changed them in a big way.

But now wasn't the time to find out precisely how.

Now was the time to run.

Spinning around on his crutches, Inchy barged through the swing-doors and limped down the corridor as fast as he could. Glancing over his shoulder, he saw that the patients were following. Questions flooded his brain. Why were they after him? Was this what happened to Mr Kowalski? But there was no time to think. He was only seconds ahead of the zombie-like crowd, which seemed to be moving faster now. Painfully, Inchy redoubled his own speed.

But the hospital corridors were like a maze. There was no way out and no help. As Inchy passed the entrance to another ward, a second crowd of patients burst forth, led by a pair of wide-eyed nurses. Inchy raced past, his crutches a blur, but more and more of them seemed to be hot on his heels.

Inchy's breath was coming in rasping gasps now. The extra weight of his plaster cast was taking its toll. He was getting tired, but his pursuers showed no signs of slowing. Gripping his crutches tighter, Inchy desperately tried to put on a fresh burst of speed as he panted round a corner.

Into a dead end.

Inchy's heart sank. Behind him he could hear the thumping footsteps of the approaching patients, but ahead of him there was no way out.

Or was there? A gleam of daylight seemed to beckon from the far end of the corridor.

Limping forward, Inchy spotted the source of the light – two emergency fire doors with glass windows. He was going to make it! Summoning the last of his strength, Inchy dragged himself over to the doors and reached for the handle.

It was too high.

Inchy felt like crying. Where was House when you really needed his big, lumbering, clumsy frame? Inchy would have forgiven him *two* broken legs if he had been there at that moment. Behind him the noise of the stumbling patients grew ever closer.

With a sigh, Inchy tipped back his head for one last glimpse of daylight. The tiny windows that had briefly offered him a hope of escape now seemed to taunt him with a vision of the outside world just beyond his reach. He could see everything – the bright blue sky, the little white fluffy clouds . . . and House's grinning face peering in at him.

Inchy couldn't believe his eyes. He'd never been so glad to see anybody.

'House!' he shouted. 'House! Help!'

House's mouth moved in reply, but Inchy couldn't hear a word. The flash of relief he had felt when he saw his friend was swamped by a fresh wave of panic. If House couldn't hear him, how could Inchy tell him how much danger he was in?

He didn't need to – House could see the terror in his face and the zoned-out patients close behind him. The big angel disappeared from view for a moment. Then, without any further warning, the doors exploded inwards.

One flew off its hinges completely, spinning down the corridor towards the approaching patients, slowing their approach. The other crashed to the floor, narrowly missing Inchy. Amidst the debris sprawled House. Leaping to his feet, he hoisted Inchy into the air and leapt back through the doorway and towards a nearby bush. The next thing Inchy knew, he was surrounded by leaves, twigs and the rest of the gang.

He started to ask how on Earth they had found him, when Alex clapped a hand over Inchy's mouth. Alex's face was tight and he put a finger to his own lips.

Behind him, Cherry had an arrow strung in

her bow. For a few seconds, the only sound in their ears was the *thumpity-thump* of their own hearts beating hard and fast.

Then, suddenly, a groaning, shuffling sound began to be heard, growing louder by the second. Cautiously, the gang peered through the leaves towards the demolished fire doors. As they watched, the shambling mass of patients and nurses started to emerge. On they came, down the path, towards the gang's hiding place.

House drew a deep breath and clenched his fists. Cherry tautened her bowstring. Even Spit looked ready for a scrap.

And the patients walked straight past.

Inchy looked at Alex, confusion clear in his eyes. Alex shrugged and shrank back further into the cover of the bush. More and more patients shuffled past, their slippered feet passing just centimetres from the gang's hiding place. Finally, as the last figure disappeared from view, everyone let out a long breath of relief.

'But they must've seen us,' hissed Inchy in disbelief. 'I mean, how could they not have noticed House pick me up and throw me in a bush? It's impossible!'

'You'd think it was impossible to demolish a set of fire doors completely, but it seems House proved us wrong,' said Spit.

'It really was pretty impressive,' agreed Alex, looking over to House with a glint in his eye. 'But I bet they didn't teach you that at the Academy.'

'No, I kind of made it up myself,' grinned House proudly.

'Well, it was totally brilliant,' said Cherry.

House shrugged. 'I guess,' he said. 'It was a split-second decision – instinct more than anything. You'd have done the same.'

'Yeah, but I'd have bounced off the doors,' laughed Cherry. 'Just as well you ate all Mrs Kowalski's cakes, really!'

Inchy poked his head out of the bush and looked down the path in the direction the patients had taken. 'Where do you think they're heading?'

'Can't say that I care,' said Spit.

'We've got to find out!' declared Inchy, hauling himself on to his crutches and out of the bush. 'They've got to be going somewhere. Adonis must have something planned for them.'

'What's Adonis got to do with this?' asked Cherry.

'He's behind it,' Inchy explained. 'He's got the patients and nurses under some form of hypnosis. When they listen to *Brain Dead* it somehow takes control of them. I don't know how it works, but I saw it happen. *Brain Dead* turned normal patients into those strange things we just saw.'

'Whoa!' whistled House.

'Quite,' replied Spit. 'And whatever our friend Adonis is up to, there's more than a whiff of demonic activity to it.'

Quickly, Alex and Spit told the rest of the gang about the picture of Adonis's radio studio in the paper, and how they'd spotted the *Necronomicon* on the shelf.

'So Adonis is in league with the Other Side,' muttered Cherry. 'That makes sense. But why is he hypnotizing the patients? What's it all for?'

'There's only one way to find out,' said Alex. 'We have to follow them.'

'Oh, great.' Spit rolled his eyes. 'Another brilliant plan from the Master of Disaster.'

'Alex is right,' snapped Cherry. 'We have to discover what they're doing. It might be the only way to find Mr Kowalski.'

'And Jim,' added Inchy. 'I made friends with

him yesterday,' he explained as the others looked at him blankly. 'But when I woke up this morning, he'd vanished too.'

'What are we waiting for, then?' cried Alex. 'Follow those patients!'

Spit rolled his eyes in exasperation, but even he followed the gang as they quickly and quietly made their way across the hospital car park, keeping an eye out for the strange parade of patients.

'There!' whispered House, spotting the last few figures as they disappeared into the corner of the car park.

'But that's a dead end,' said Alex. 'There's nothing there at all.'

'Well, they don't seem to think so,' said Inchy. 'Look, it's not a dead end – there's a gap in the fence.'

Suddenly, Cherry stopped walking. 'Oh no.'

'Cherry?' asked Inchy, turning. 'What's wrong?'

'It *is* a dead end,' said Cherry. 'Not in the way Alex meant, but it's certainly dead, and it's definitely the end for those who end up there.'

'Great,' said Spit, kicking a loose stone across the tarmac. 'We've got a hospitalful of patients wandering around in a state of hypnosis and now

Cherry's decided to start talking in riddles. What exactly do you mean?'

'You mentioned it yourself – how "conveniently" the hospital was located,' replied Cherry grimly. 'Don't you remember what was next door? It's the ultimate dead end – the cemetery. They're all going into Green Hill Cemetery!'

12
The Graveyard Shift

'Now this is something you don't see every day,' said Spit as the gang edged through the gap in the fence and past some old, worn tombstones.

'Really?' replied Cherry. 'I thought all hospitals gave their patients exercise by sending them out under hypnosis to wander around graveyards!'

'But what are they up to?' asked Alex, pushing forward through the undergrowth to get a better look.

'Ouch!' said Cherry. 'Watch where you're putting your feet, you . . .'

Cherry's voice tailed off, but it didn't matter, Alex wasn't listening anyway. He was staring.

'What's up?' called House in a low voice. 'Why've we stopped?'

'Yeah, come on, Alex,' said Spit, 'don't hog the view.'

The rest of the gang pushed forward to join Alex and Cherry at the edge of a tangle of overgrown bushes. Now, just a few metres away, they could finally see clearly what the patients were doing.

They were digging.

Still in their hospital gowns and pyjamas, teams of patients stood around dozens of graves, relentlessly burrowing down, down, down. Dust and grit spun high into the air as they used their bare hands to pull stones and roots free from the grip of the earth.

They also pulled up coffins. On one side of the graveyard, two piles of them towered high, and more were being added every minute. Some were new, the brass handles still shiny. Others looked ancient, close to disintegrating into dust. And at the centre of it all, commanding the show like some gothic circus ringmaster, stood Aubrey Adonis.

His hands were outstretched, the fingers splayed outwards. Occasionally, a spark of blue light would crackle and fizz from them and dart around the graveyard like lightning. Whenever it touched patients, they jumped and moved faster, as if energized.

Adonis's face was wild, his eyes close to bursting from his face, his smile a slash of thin lips and ferocious teeth. Above the graveyard, a dark sky bubbled and boiled like hot mud. Light itself seemed to be avoiding the place, as though it was horrified by what it had seen and wanted to forget about it very quickly indeed.

'Oh my,' croaked Inchy. 'I think I've been here before.'

'*What?!*' hissed Spit incredulously. 'And you didn't think to tell us that before now?'

'I don't remember it,' replied Inchy, 'but when I woke up this morning I noticed that I had dirty hands. Loads of other people did too. It didn't make any sense then, but now . . .'

'Well, this pretty much seals the deal on Adonis, doesn't it?' said Alex. 'I mean, I'm no lawyer, but I think that what we see before us is enough to convince anyone that he's not really a hospital radio DJ.'

'Then what is he?' asked Cherry, still staring. 'Is he a human or is he a demon?'

'Oh, he's human,' replied Inchy slowly, 'but –'

'If he's human, then I can take him,' barked House, turning to the rest of the gang. 'Who's with me?'

No one stepped forward.

'Let me finish, House,' said Inchy. 'He may be human, but I think he's a necromancer.'

'A necro-*what*?'

'Necromancer,' explained Inchy. 'A human servant of the Other Side. They're horrible in most ways – as close as a human gets to being a demon. The "mancer" bit means they're into magic and stuff.'

'Oh no,' gulped Cherry.

'It's worse than "oh no", I'm afraid,' continued Inchy. 'The "necro" bit? Well, that means "dead". Necromancers use the dark magic of death and the dead.'

'Not very nice, then?' said Spit.

'No,' replied Inchy. 'Not in any way.'

'Where do you learn all this stuff?' asked House.

'From books,' said Inchy. 'You should try one sometime.'

'OK, so Adonis is a necromancer,' said House. He chewed his lip for a moment, then brightened. 'But it could be worse — at least there aren't any zombies, although those patients are doing quite a good impression!'

'A good point and well made,' said Spit, 'but from now on I would suggest that you don't make any more.'

'But we've got to do something!' said House. 'We can't just stand by and let him dig up people's graves. I don't need Gabriel to tell me that's not right.'

'You're right: we can't ignore this,' agreed Alex. 'But what *can* we do? If Adonis has magic powers, we don't stand much of a chance.'

'Alex, look!' hissed Cherry, pointing.

'Where are they going?'

The gang watched as, at a gesture from Adonis, the patients stopped digging and started to make their way back towards the hospital. Most were returning just as they had come out, only muddier. Others, though, were going back with something they hadn't brought with them.

'They're taking the coffins back in with them!' Cherry's eyes bulged at the thought.

'I'd prefer a hot water bottle,' said House.

Ducking back into the cover of the bushes, they watched as Adonis ordered the hypnotized digging party back through the gap in the fence. Keeping low, Alex led the gang in pursuit.

In the car park, the patients split into two groups. One went back in through the broken fire doors, obviously heading straight for their wards. The other group, the ones carrying the coffins, turned left towards a small metal door, with Adonis in the lead. As the door clanged shut behind them, the gang scurried up. Without hesitation, Alex reached for the handle.

'Hold on a minute,' said Cherry, slapping his hand away. 'Call me superstitious, but I don't much like the look of this. The last time we decided to see what the bad guy was doing behind a mysterious door, didn't we end up in a battle with a Level Four Fire Demon?'

'And that was big, big trouble,' declared House.

'You mean you didn't enjoy it?' asked Spit, smirking.

'Come on, that wasn't the same,' said Alex, gripping the handle. 'Ouch!'

He pulled his hand back sharply. 'It *really* wasn't the same,' he hissed, sticking his hand under his armpit. 'Dante's cellar was boiling hot. That door's freezing! It's so cold, it burns!'

'Now that you mention it,' said Inchy, rubbing his hands together briskly, 'it's pretty cold just standing here.'

It was true. It wasn't just the door that was freezing cold but the very air around them. Their breath hung in clouds, as if it was the middle of winter rather than summer. Within a matter of seconds, the whole team was shivering.

'L-l-look,' chattered Spit, 'l-let's just get this over w-with, OK?'

'B-but we don't know w-what's in there,' objected Cherry, jiggling up and down on the spot.

'Well, I'd r-rather take my chance with a

n–necromancer than f–freeze to death. Which is what's going to happen if we s-stay here.'

'Come on, then,' said House, and before anyone could stop him, he pushed open the door and marched through.

The gang followed him inside and stopped dead, staring at the sight before them. It looked as if they were in what had once been a storeroom – until it was hit by a blizzard. The place was utterly frozen. Icicles hung glittering from the light bulbs and the windows were thick with frost. Ice cascaded over a pile of old chairs, like a frozen waterfall. Everything was covered in sparkling whiteness. It looked strangely beautiful, like a scene from a fairy tale.

Only instead of fairies, there were coffins. Piles and piles of coffins – filling the room, lying on the floor, stacked up against the wall. Some were partly encrusted in the ice, while others were laid neatly on top of it.

'There must be hundreds of them,' said Alex, wide-eyed. He was so shocked, his teeth had forgotten to chatter. 'What's going on?'

'It's Adonis,' said Inchy. 'He's made this happen.'

'How?' asked Spit, holding his hand out, palm upwards. 'I mean, look – it's actually *snowing* in here!'

'He's using magic to keep it cold so he can store the bodies.'

'Why?'

'To stop them going off until he's ready to bring them to life as zombies,' said Inchy, looking more than a little queasy.

'Blimey,' muttered House. 'So there *are* zombies. There's enough of them here for an army!'

And as House spoke, everything clicked into place in Inchy's mind. His brain rewound back to the words he had heard through the door of Adonis's studio – *One more day and you will have all the soldiers that you need.*

'That's it!' exclaimed Inchy. 'It *is* an army. Adonis is building an army of zombies! He's using *Brain Dead* to hypnotize the patients to dig up the bodies, and when he has enough, he'll bring them to life and use them to take over Green Hill!'

The gang stood stunned. The diabolical genius of Adonis was enough to take their breath away.

'We have to stop him,' said Alex finally. 'There must be a way for the patients to get back into the main part of the hospital from here.' He scanned the room. Its shape barely visible through the strange indoor snowstorm, Alex could just make out another door. 'There it is! Come on!'

Without a second thought, the gang raced forward, dodging coffins and ducking under hanging icicles. Unfortunately, the ice-covered floor meant that racing forward was much easier than stopping.

As they found when they approached the double doors.

House lost his balance, landing on his bottom with a thump that knocked the air out of him. Arms windmilling, Alex tripped over his big friend, sending Cherry and Spit flying too. Only Inchy, stabilized by his crutches, managed to stay on his feet as the gang crashed through the doors in a tumble of flying limbs and rude words.

From his position at the bottom of the pile, House was the first to notice their new surroundings.

'Kitchen!' he said. 'We're in the kitchen!'

The rest of the gang pulled themselves up on to their feet and looked around. They were surrounded by the gleam of metal surfaces – pots and pans, cookers, worktops and shelves of tins.

Slowly, they started to edge their way forward. The kitchen was an enormous place filled with impossible smells, most of them deeply unpleasant. And the further they went, the worse the smells became.

'Something isn't right,' said Inchy nervously.

'Too right,' said House. 'I've tried the food they make in here – it's rubbish.'

'Yes, but *who* made the food?' said Spit. 'If this is a kitchen, where are the chefs?'

'Um, here they are,' replied Cherry, as a tall figure stepped out from behind an even taller set of shelves.

The figure was wearing a big white hat, but that was where any similarity to a real chef ended. Beneath the hat, its face was waxy and grey, with empty eye sockets and a long scar that ran all the way across its throat. Its toothy mouth grinned death and decay. Behind the first figure, several more looked up from the saucepans they were stirring.

'Zombies,' said Spit, stating the obvious.

'Cooking the food,' said Inchy, following suit.

Cherry swallowed hard.

'Anyone for takeaway?'

13
Kitchen Nightmares

'We're dead,' said Spit.

'No, *they're* dead,' corrected Inchy.

'This is no time for jokes,' moaned House.

'No wonder the place smells so bad,' observed Alex, surveying the band of zombies facing them. Some had no hair, others had just a few wisps, half of which fell off every time they moved, taking strips of dry skin with it, dropping into the cooking pots with a revolting splash. Alex felt his stomach do a somersault. 'And I guess that's why the food is so foul.'

The zombies' clothes were like a snapshot of

history's dirty laundry. One was wearing a battered dusty top hat and carrying a broken cane. Another, which looked like the remains of a tall and elegant woman, was swooshing around in a tattered ballgown. The fabric of the dress stretched over the empty ribcage beneath it like the tired skin of a long-forgotten airship. Scampering up and down inside was a pair of large rats.

'I don't suppose you've got a plan for this sort of situation?' Cherry asked Alex, pulling out her bow.

Alex was just about to admit reluctantly that he had nothing of the sort when the zombie wearing the head chef's hat let out a strangled groan. As if this was the signal they had been waiting for, the other zombies grabbed hold of an alarming array of carving knives, cleavers and wicked-looking skewers. Armed, they began to stumble forward, blades flashing.

'You know what,' said Spit, 'I'm getting the impression they don't like us.'

'Well, the feeling's mutual,' snarled Cherry, loosing an arrow. The shaft zipped through the air and slammed straight into the eye socket of the head chef zombie and out the back of its head, pinning it to the monster behind.

'Nice shot!' yelled Alex. 'You been practising?'

The gang waited for the arrows to take effect and the zombies to turn and gaze lovingly at each other. But they didn't. Instead, with a ferocious heave, the lead zombie pulled itself forward, yanking the arrow straight through its head, leaving a hole big enough to see daylight through. Then it resumed its steady march towards them.

Another arrow fizzed through the air, followed by another and another. At such close range, even Cherry's notoriously dodgy aim was good enough to pepper the leading zombies. But they didn't even slow down.

'What's wrong?' asked Spit, as the gang started to back away.

'I don't think my arrows work on zombies. Being dead kind of stops people falling in love.'

'Right!' yelled House, eyes afire. 'I've had enough of this!' He turned, reached into a draw and pulled out a weapon of his own. Everyone gasped.

'What is *that*?' squeaked Cherry.

'I think . . .' replied House, looking at the strange device in his hand, '. . . it's an electric whisk. Hey, no fair! How come they get all the sharp stuff?'

Nobody had time to answer House's question, though, as a terrible roar erupted from the zombies. The monsters broke into a shambling run, brandishing their knives as they stumbled towards the gang.

'We have to immobilize them,' cried Inchy.

House looked blank.

'Stop them moving!' Spit explained in a shriek.

'Oh right,' nodded House. 'You mean smash 'em up!'

'Exactly! Grab anything you can!' yelled Alex. 'And chuck it!'

No one needed to be told twice. House hurled the electric whisk at the nearest zombie. Alex and Spit upended a huge saucepan of foul-smelling liquid on to the floor, trying to prevent the other zombies getting any closer. Cherry and Inchy slung kettles and frying pans.

But it wasn't enough. The advancing zombies just seemed to ignore the barrage of kitchen weaponry.

'It's not working!' yelled Inchy, as the zombies spread out across the kitchen.

'They've cut off our exit!' hollered Spit. 'We're trapped!'

Alex's stomach lurched. It was true – without seeming to do so, the zombies had backed them into a corner.

'Do something, Alex!' pleaded Cherry. 'We've thrown everything at them except the kitchen sink.'

Alex's reply died on his lips as a strange shadow fell over him. What new monster was this? It was large, black and square, and it looked like it had legs . . .

'Forget the kitchen sink,' grunted a strained voice. 'I've got a better idea!'

'That's not possible,' said Spit, mouth open, eyes popping.

'I don't think House agrees,' replied Inchy.

Sweat pouring from his forehead, Big House lumbered forward, his huge frame towering over the gang. Held high above his head was an enormous silver fridge. With an almighty heave, he launched it towards the zombies.

As the fridge came crashing down, it exploded like a bomb. The door flew off, flattening two zombies. The contents of the fridge bounced out, causing two others to trip up. And the fridge itself ploughed on, sending zombies flying like skittles.

For a moment, silence settled over the kitchen like a shroud.

Then, slowly, with the twitch of a head and the stretching of an arm, the zombies rose from the destruction.

'It's like there's someone controlling them or something,' muttered Alex. 'They just won't give up!'

'That's it!' yelled Inchy. 'Someone's controlling them! Adonis! There's no other explanation! Listen, guys –!'

But before Inchy had a chance to finish, a zombie wearing an oversized dusty grey wig loomed out from behind some shelves and grabbed hold of him. Alex and Spit leapt forward and clung on to Inchy's legs, but they weren't quick enough. The remaining zombies had seized him too.

Thrashing desperately, Inchy felt himself being torn away from his friends. It was like he was in a tug of war – but as the rope. Clammy hands pawed at him and tugged at his clothes and face. One of his crutches snapped with a splintering crunch. He screamed, but it was useless – the zombies had him. He was about to be dragged to a sticky death. A hideous zombie face loomed closer and closer, as if it was about to bite his nose off . . .

And then it exploded, sliced in two by what looked like a metal spatula. As Inchy watched, amazed, the remaining zombies holding him were torn apart, ripped to shreds by a lightning-fast blur.

As the zombies fell back, the blur slowed down until it became the figure of a thin old man wearing ripped pyjamas, with a red bandana tied around his forehead. He was clutching a ladle in one hand and a baking tray in the other.

Inchy stared. 'You!'

'I heard ze noises and here I am. Up you get, yes?'

Mr Kowalski pulled Inchy to his feet. 'You ver vondering vere I had gone?'

As Inchy opened his mouth to reply, a zombie reared up behind Mr Kowalski. A huge cleaver gleamed in the light . . .

Without even looking, Mr Kowalski spun round and sliced the zombie's head off with the baking tray. The head landed with a dull thump some way off, a look of surprise on its cold grey features.

'I vill explain later,' said Mr Kowalski. 'First ve must be finishing off ze zombies, yes? Ve haven't got much time!'

The rest of the gang dashed forward.

'Do you know how to defeat them?' asked Cherry breathlessly.

'Simple.' Mr Kowalski eyed each of the team in turn. 'You heff to chop zem into teeny tiny pieces!'

House grinned widely. 'Of course! I remember reading about it in my Guardian Angel manual. Cutting their heads off works best.'

'Yes!' agreed Mr Kowalski, nodding vigorously. 'Off vis ze heads!' And he sprinted towards the zombies, yelling a blood-curdling battle cry.

'Cool!' said House. 'Now I can use my sliding tackle again!' With that, he charged forward, slid low and smacked into an unfortunate zombie hard and fast. The monster flew into the air, its legs coming free from its body and shooting across the kitchen in opposite directions.

'Just be glad that wasn't you yesterday,' said Spit to Inchy.

'Oh, I am.'

As House and Mr Kowalski took on the zombies hand to hand, Inchy prowled the edge of the kitchen, hurling missiles at any that tried to escape. He was aiming at their faces, and one zombie had its head knocked clean off by a huge tin of tomatoes.

'Duck!' yelled Alex as the head zoomed towards Cherry. It dropped at her feet.

'If I was the screaming type,' said Cherry, looking down at the rather grisly sight, 'I would probably scream about now. But as I'm not . . .'

With a deft flick of her left foot, Cherry chipped the head high up into the air. It hung there just long enough for its one remaining eye to plop out and its mouth to let out a small moan. Then Cherry leapt backwards and executed a perfect overhead kick, bringing her right foot round in an arc to connect with the head.

With a horrid empty thud, like someone hitting a large coconut with a wooden mallet, the head shot off across the kitchen. It went straight through the stomach of one zombie and knocked the head off the one behind it, before coming to rest in a frying pan.

Now Alex and Spit crashed into the melee. For once they seemed to be working together, grabbing hold of a zombie's arms and tugging in opposite directions, like pulling a Christmas cracker, until the monster split into two down the middle.

Finally, House dispatched the last of the zombies with a hefty punch. Its head landed with a splat in one of the cooking pots, narrowly missing covering House from head to toe in the revolting gunk.

'Vell,' said Mr Kowalski, 've have von ze battle but not ze war.'

Inchy turned to him, a measuring jug hanging limply from his hand. 'You saved us,' he said. 'But what happened to you? Where did you go? I came to look for you, but you were gone.'

Mr Kowalski smiled. 'You remember ven I

showed you zat cotton vool in my headphones, yes?'

Inchy nodded, as the rest of the gang gathered round.

'Ze nurses, zey found out vot I voz doing, so I vent on ze run!' Mr Kowalski's eyes shone.

'But where to?' asked Cherry.

'Here in ze hospital!' said Mr Kowalski. 'I have been hiding in ze old operating theatres, in ze basement, here in ze kitchen. It voz just like old times for me – lying low and spying on ze enemy. I've never felt so alive!'

'You were right,' said Inchy. 'About this hospital, I mean. Something evil's at work here.'

'And I know vot it is,' said Mr Kowalski.

'Adonis,' said Inchy. 'He's controlling the zombies.'

Mr Kowalski nodded. 'Exactly.'

Suddenly, an electronic crackle buzzed through the air like an angry wasp. Then there was a howl of feedback as the hospital tannoy system burst into life. Then a laugh. A deep, rumbling sickly-sweet laugh that rolled down the corridors like thunder.

'Impressive, very impressive,' said a voice they

all recognized. Adonis. 'I must say, I was rather taken by surprise by your antics. Yes, very impressive. Particularly the hero-to-the-rescue scene at the end. I almost cried. Almost.'

He paused. 'Yes, "the end". Which is where you all are now, I'm afraid.' Adonis laughed again, but this time it was an insane laugh, high-pitched and shrill. 'During my time in this revolting little hospital, all you pathetic patients have been under the impression that I cared about you. That I wanted to bring you comfort and peace and healing. But you were wrong. Oh, how terribly, deliciously wrong!

'You see,' he continued, 'I'm not what you would exactly call your average DJ. After all, how many normal DJs know how to use a radio show to hypnotize people into digging up an army of the dead, hmm? And now my army is complete I have no more need of you. You will be the first victims of my brilliant scheme.'

Adonis laughed again. Then spoke a command in a booming voice. 'Now, awake, my children! Awake!'

A rumbling sound rippled through the air, thumping like a giant disembodied heartbeat.

From the other side of the kitchen wall, a hundred voices moaned in response.

'You know that storeroom where it was snowing?' said Spit. 'The one very full of dead people?'

The gang nodded dumbly.

'I think it's about to become very empty.'

14
Radio Ga-Ga

'We've got to stop this!'

'And the prize for stating the blatantly obvious goes to . . . Alex!'

'Look, Spit,' said Alex. 'You heard Adonis. If we don't do something, the zombies will kill the patients and then overrun the town. It's up to us to prevent it!'

'But we only just survived against those zombie chefs. We don't stand a chance against a whole army!' exclaimed Cherry.

As if in agreement, the door to the storeroom

shuddered as a horrifying zombie moan echoed through the air.

'Adonis must be using the hospital radio system to amplify his powers somehow,' said Inchy. 'It's the only way he can control so many zombies.'

'I have ze idea,' said Mr Kowalski. 'Ve split up. You go get Adonis. I'll hold off ze zombies.'

'On your own?' said Spit. 'How on Earth will you do that?'

Wordlessly, Mr Kowalski reached into the nearest drawer and produced two strange and fearsome-looking kitchen utensils.

'Wow!' gawped House. 'Spiky hammers!'

'They're for tenderizing meat,' said Inchy.

'I knew that,' lied House.

Before anyone could raise any other objections to the plan, the storeroom doors burst inwards under the weight of a squirming mass of the dead. Mr Kowalski looked at the gang and winked. Then, yelling something in Polish that sounded very rude, he charged into the ranks of zombies, smashing right and left. Soon bits of zombie were flying everywhere.

'Brave,' said Inchy.

'Insane,' said Spit.

'Right, where's the radio studio?' asked Alex.

Inchy pointed with his one remaining crutch. 'On the third floor. But I can't run anywhere like this.'

'Allow me,' said House, swinging Inchy on to his back. 'Now hold on!' Then he charged down the corridor, Inchy on his back, like a strange vision of a medieval knight with a crutch instead of a lance.

The gang followed, racing through the hospital, past small knots of bleary-eyed patients. Freed from the influence of *Brain Dead* they were confused and disorientated.

Inchy recognized one. 'Stop!' he yelled. 'Stop!'

House skidded to a halt.

'Lily, it's Inchy. You have to go back to your ward. Take the others and barricade yourselves in, OK?'

Lily rubbed her eyes. 'Where am I, Inchy? How did I get out of bed? Where's my knitting?'

'It's in your ward,' said Inchy, his voice firm. 'You'll be safe there. Trust me, Lily.'

Lily looked bemused. 'Of course I trust you, Inchy.'

'Good. I'll see you soon.'

Racing to catch up with the others, it wasn't long before they were all outside the radio studio.

'Ready?' panted Alex.

'Ready!' chorused the gang.

House — with Inchy still on his back — barged through the door, with Alex, Spit and Cherry right behind.

It was like falling into a black hole. Inside, the studio was utterly dark. But it was a darkness that was more than just the absence of light — it was everywhere and everything. It dripped from the ceiling, treacle-thick, making it hard to breathe. For a long second the gang stood motionless, wondering if at any moment the darkness would close its fist and crush them into nothingness.

Then, painfully slowly, their eyes adjusted. The room wasn't empty — machinery grew out of the gloom. Alex could see a large desk covered with volume knobs, sockets for electric leads and lots of little LED lights. It looked like it might once have been the controls for the radio station, but now it seemed almost alive. Plastic buttons had transformed into claws, and levers into strange bone-like rods. The tiny lights blinked like eyes. Cables draped the walls and snaked across the floor like veins. Everything was connected to everything else and the whole thing glistened and pulsed slowly, like a huge heart.

'Oh no,' said Inchy, sliding off House's back.

'What?' asked Cherry.

Ignoring her, Inchy pointed to a thick red cable on the floor. 'House?' he called. 'Do you reckon you could snap this?'

'No worries,' said House, gripping the cable in both hands.

'Don't be an idiot!' yelled Spit. 'That's electric!'

'No, it isn't,' said Inchy. 'Do it, House!' And before anyone could do anything about it, House ripped it in two.

A red spray licked over them like a huge tongue.

'Wow!' said House. 'What is that?'

'Blood,' said Inchy, his voice horrible and cold.

'Blood!' squealed Cherry, brushing crimson

droplets from her arm. 'Why? Where's it from? What's it for?'

'This is a hospital,' said Inchy. 'There's bound to be a blood bank somewhere. Adonis is using it to power this machine.'

'Impossible,' spluttered Alex.

'All servants of the Other Side need blood to work whatever evil it is they're up to,' said Inchy. 'Adonis has combined magic with technology. It's brilliant – in a terrible way.'

Cherry looked like she was going to throw up. 'It's foul,' she groaned. 'Adonis is really, really sick.'

'And there he is,' pointed House.

The rest of the gang turned. In the far wall of the room was a large window beside a thick glass door that led into the inner studio. Behind it stood the tall figure of Aubrey Adonis.

'There's someone with him,' said Cherry.

'It's Jim!' yelled Inchy. 'He's got Jim!'

It was true. Adonis was clutching the boy against him, one thin arm wrapped round his shoulders. Jim's eyes were glassy and he stared straight ahead, unseeing.

Adonis smiled wickedly, the nerves in his

cheeks twitching. His face was like a billowing black cloud, laced with flashes of lightning. Looking at him was like staring into the eye of a storm. Then he raised his empty hand and an arc of blazing blue pulsed through the air from his outstretched fingers. It melted through the window, burning a perfect hole, missed the gang by nothing but luck, and slammed into a filing cabinet, which burst into flames.

The gang hurled themselves to the floor.

'We're dead,' choked Spit.

'Well, at least we won't be alone,' said Cherry as, from outside the studio, the distant sound of moaning zombies cut through the air.

But Inchy didn't hear them. Or the words of his friends either, for that matter. His mind was in another place entirely. He was staring at Adonis and he suddenly knew that there was nothing he wouldn't do to rescue Jim. His role as an angel, its very meaning, was utterly clear – to protect.

Adonis chuckled horribly and raised his hand to blaze magical lightning at the gang once more. The blue crackle blistered the air, riding the echo of Adonis's laughter. Spit, Cherry, Alex and

House dived for cover behind various parts of Adonis's hideous blood-fuelled control desk.

Inchy dived in the other direction. Towards Adonis.

The neat round hole burned in the glass by Adonis's lightning was all Inchy could see. It was very small . . . but then so was he. With a superhuman effort, Inchy flung himself through the air.

The gang gasped, their breath stuck fast in their throats, as Inchy scraped the sides of the hole and was through, his crutch clattering on the floor in front of him.

For a moment, the gang were dumbstruck. Then Alex sprang into life.

'Get in there after him!' he cried.

In a flash, House was up and at the glass door that led into the inner studio, with the others in hot pursuit. They all had Adonis in their sights. House gripped the handle and pulled. Nothing happened. He pulled again. 'Alex! It won't budge!'

From the corridor came another rattling moan.

'The zombies are coming!' gasped Cherry.

'Thanks for the heads-up!' said Spit, who didn't look particularly thankful.

House shook the door. Kicked it. Punched it. Nothing. 'It's too strong!' he yelled.

'Just a minute,' hissed Alex, pulling out something that he'd had hanging round his neck, hidden under his sweater.

'You're joking,' said Spit, looking at the bag in Alex's hand. It was the Lucky Dip.

Cherry couldn't believe it either. 'We haven't got time for this,' she said as Alex tugged Tabbris's fishing rod out of the bag. 'For goodness' sake, Alex,' she screamed. 'I don't think we need a Demon Tester to tell us that Adonis is evil!'

'I'm not going to use it to test anything,' Alex snarled. 'I need this!'

'A fishing hook,' observed Spit. 'How useful.'

A horrifying moan echoed from just outside the studio.

'Look, get out of my way,' snapped Alex. 'House – keep that other door shut! Cherry, Spit – find something to use as a weapon.'

'But what are you doing?' asked Spit.

Alex dropped to his knees. 'How do you think

I was always able to get out of Gabriel's locked office?'

'With a fish hook?' answered Cherry incredulously.

Alex smiled tightly and poked the hook into the keyhole. He'd never encountered a lock he couldn't pick.

Then again, he'd never tried to do it with an army of zombies at the door . . .

On the other side of the glass, Inchy hobbled into the shadow of the towering figure of Adonis.

At his side stood Jim, eyes blank and lost. Behind him lay another control desk – the one that Adonis was clearly using to control the zombies. Like the machinery in the outer room, it was a strange mix of the technological and the arcane. It pulsated with unholy life, flickers of blue energy crawling all over it. The air was heavy with the smell of brimstone.

Outside the studio, the rumbling moan of the approaching zombies grew steadily louder. From out of the corner of his eye, Inchy could see House pressed hard against the studio door, desperately holding it shut. Spit and Cherry were ransacking the outer room in search of weapons, terror ripe in their eyes. Alex was crouched by the glass door, trying to do something with the lock to get to Inchy.

Inchy swallowed hard. Right now, he was on his own.

Adonis smiled. 'Are you enjoying the show, Inchy?'

'Show's over, Adonis,' Inchy replied, hoping he sounded braver than he felt.

'On the contrary, my little friend,' sneered Adonis. 'It's only just begun.' Adonis turned to Jim and ruffled his hair. Inchy squirmed at the sight. 'Dear little Jim,' Adonis crooned. 'So innocent, so perfect.'

'What do you want him for?' said Inchy.

'Silly boy,' hissed Adonis. 'It's his blood I want, not him.'

'But you've got blood in that machine already,' yelled Inchy. 'It's what you're using to control the zombies, isn't it? Why do you need more?'

'That's *old* blood,' said Adonis. 'And I need it young and fresh. The final ingredient that will make my control of the zombies permanent.'

Inchy went pale. 'But you can't! It's . . . it's —'

'Wrong? Evil? Slightly naughty?' Adonis sneered, his gold teeth glinting. 'Well, yes, it is, Inchy. But there's not much you can do about it really, is there?'

The twisted DJ snapped out his hand, releasing a bolt of sizzling power. Inchy hurled himself to the left. As he rolled aside, just escaping the lightning, his broken leg shot a wave of agony into his brain.

'Such a shame about your leg,' gloated Adonis. 'If you didn't have that cast, you might have been able to save your little friend. But as it is . . .'

Reaching out a long arm, Adonis picked Jim up with one hand. 'I'm sorry I can't give you longer to say goodbye,' he giggled madly, 'but when I'm finished with little Jimmy here, I think I might just have time to impale you on that crutch of yours. How delicious!'

With a final insane cackle, Adonis lifted Jim high into the air over the control desk and raised his other hand, blue lightning crackling around his fingertips.

But Inchy's mind was faster. As soon as Adonis

had mentioned his cast and his crutch, Inchy knew what to do. As the necromancer raised his hand, Inchy sprang forward, grabbing the crutch and using it to propel him into the air like someone doing a pole vault.

Higher and higher he flew, until he was almost face-to-face with Adonis. Then, twisting his body in mid-air, Inchy kicked out with all his strength. His plastered leg crashed into the side of Adonis's head with a *thwack* that sounded like a whale being dropped from a helicopter on to a tennis court.

With a scream, the stunned DJ dropped Jim to the floor and staggered backwards, clutching his face. Inchy thumped to the ground next to Jim, winded.

'Enough playing!' screeched Adonis. 'It is time for you all to die.'

He clapped his hands sharply and, in a ripple of blue lightning, his body crackled, shimmered and disappeared. A second later, Inchy saw House stagger backwards as the studio door exploded. In the corridor beyond, Adonis reappeared at the head of his zombie army.

'Feast upon them!' he screamed, his nose

squashed into a very odd shape from Inchy's kick. 'Tear them apart and feed!'

Stumbling and gnashing their teeth, the zombies lurched forward.

'We're done for!' yelled Spit. 'We're trapped!'

'Get that door open, Alex!' bellowed Cherry.

CLICK!

'Yes!'

To everyone's surprise, the lock opened and Alex fell into the inner studio.

'You lot – in here now!' called Inchy as Spit, Cherry and House bolted inside. House slammed the door behind them and pinned himself to it, a huge, immovable wedge. Like a tidal wave, the zombies flooded into the outer room. Soon a sea of rotting faces was squashed up against the glass, staring in at them.

'I'm not sure how long I can hold this,' groaned House, trying to ignore the leering zombies only millimetres away.

'Inchy!' called Alex, looking at the control desk. 'See if any of those buttons can break the link between Adonis and the zombies. We need to shut this down!'

Hobbling painfully, Inchy crossed to the desk, flicking and pushing every switch he could see. 'It's not working!' he yelled. 'It's not working!'

'I'm losing it!' shouted House. 'I can't hold on!'

Suddenly, inspiration struck Spit. If the zombies were all tuned in to the radio, then maybe they could use that against them!

Pushing past Inchy, he seized something from the control desk. 'Cherry!' he shouted. 'Here!'

Cherry turned to find a microphone thrust in front of her. 'This isn't really the time for karaoke, Spit,' she fumed.

'It's just the time,' said Spit. 'Now sing!'

'But –' protested Cherry.

'*Sing!*'

With a shrug, Cherry opened her mouth and shattered the air with a note so wrong, so twisted and broken, that it cut through the wall of zombie noise like the shriek of nails down a blackboard. Outside, the zombies hesitated.

'What are you doing?' shouted Alex.

'Seeing just how destructive Cherry's singing really is!' Spit yelled back. 'But we need more volume! Crank it up to ten!'

Inchy reached across and turned everything up full. Cherry took a deep breath and let out such a screeching chorus that Spit thought his brain would melt. Inside the studio, a light bulb and two glasses of water exploded.

'They're backing off!' called House.

'Keep going, Cherry!' encouraged Spit. 'Your voice is driving them back!'

'You saying I can't sing?' snapped Cherry angrily.

'Don't stop or we're all dead, got it?' Spit replied.

'But —'

'SING!'

'Fine!' yelled Cherry. 'I *will*!'

Cherry's next note was like the sound of a thousand cats being slowly strangled. The studio window cracked. The walls shook. Alex and Inchy fell to the floor, hands wrapped round their heads, trying to shut out the din. House stared as the glass door he'd been holding disintegrated.

Through the doorway, he saw the zombies staggering and falling over each other, all desperately trying to cover their ears. And then, with a series of gunshot-loud *cracks*, their heads exploded.

Silence.

For the next few seconds, bits of zombie fell like rain, covering the floor in a corpse carpet. Then, with a sound like water draining down a plughole, the bodies started to crumble and dissolve, until all that was left was dust. Then that vanished too. A moment later, nothing was left of the zombies at all.

15
Discharged

'Well, *that* I wasn't expecting,' said House, staring around incredulously.

'How's Jim, Inchy?' asked Alex, looking over to where the smaller angel was supporting the boy.

'He's still unconscious, but I think he's going to be OK. Hopefully he won't remember anything.'

Cherry gazed at their surroundings in a daze. Daylight could be seen through a wide crack in one of the walls, and a large section of the ceiling had collapsed. 'Did my voice do all that?'

Alex nodded. 'I'm afraid so. You've got a unique voice, Cherry. I don't think you'll be winning any talent shows, but it certainly came in handy today!'

'Erm, I hate to rain on your parade, guys,' interrupted Spit, 'but where's Adonis? Cherry's singing destroyed the zombies because they were connected up to the radio transmitter, but Adonis wasn't. He might still be out there!'

Alex slapped a hand to his forehead. 'You're right! We've got to get after him!'

At that moment, Mr Kowalski's head popped round the door. 'No need, no need. Ve heff everything under control, see?'

Out in the corridor stood Adonis, bound head to toe with bandages and plaster-tape, and surrounded by a group of very awake and very angry patients. Lily was standing guard, furiously knitting a pair of handcuffs.

'Ven I had finished off ze zombies in ze kitchen, I came looking for you,' said Mr Kowalski. 'Zen I found Lily fighting off some other zombies in my old ward, so I joined ze struggle. Ve had almost lost, but zen ze zombies suddenly start exploding! Zen ve ran up to ze studio and here is Adonis trying to get avay! So ve grabbed him!'

Adonis looked across to the gang, eyes dark with hatred. 'Don't think this is finished, children. You've won a battle, that's all. But this is a war, you understand? A war. And my master will wreak revenge on you, the like of which you could never imagine in your worst nightmares.'

'Come on, you,' snapped Mr Kowalski. 'Ze police are waiting to ask you a few questions.' And with that, he hauled Adonis away.

'He doesn't look happy, does he?' chuckled House.

'No,' agreed Spit. 'But then I'm guessing that his plans for taking over the world with an army of zombies didn't include the bit about him getting arrested.'

The gang were standing outside the hospital watching a bedraggled Adonis being led away by some very confused policemen. Everywhere was chaos. Fire engines were spraying water into the third floor, trying to put out the small fires started by Adonis's lightning. In the car park, doctors and nurses milled about, trying to help the confused patients.

Adonis pushed and pulled against the police and managed to turn to face the gang. 'You meddling kids!' he yelled, foaming at the mouth with fury. 'You'll regret what you've done here! When my master –'

His voice was cut off as a particularly large and tough-looking policeman bundled him into the back of a police car.

'There it is again,' muttered Alex quietly.

'There what is?' replied Cherry.

'Well, first we have to deal with Dante the demon, then it's Adonis the necromancer. And we heard *both* of them talking to someone they called "master". And what about the other fun stuff like Dante's imps and the zombies! There's definitely something majorly demonic going on in this town.'

'But why would demons want to come to a quiet little town in the middle of nowhere?' asked House.

'Perhaps because it seems so unlikely,' suggested Inchy. 'Green Hill is the last place on Earth you'd expect to find agents of the Other Side – so that's precisely why they've come here. To get the element of surprise.'

'But what are they doing here?' mused Alex.

Before any of them had a chance to respond, a figure appeared at their side, quivering with rage.

'Tabbris!' said Alex. 'Er, hi. How are you?'

'How am I?' Tabbris snapped. 'I am fine. Which is more than can be said for these poor people whose hospital you have almost single-handedly destroyed!'

Everyone stared hard at the ground.

'So what exactly has been going on?' Tabbris continued.

'Well,' said House, wondering where to begin, 'it all sort of just kicked off –'

'"Kicked off"?' interrupted Tabbris. '*Kicked off!* Was this something to do with football again?'

'No,' replied Alex hotly. 'It was to do with Aubrey Adonis – he's a necromancer!'

Tabbris's eyes bulged. 'What rot. I've spoken to the policeman in charge and he says that five children – you – have apparently caused some sort of explosion in the hospital radio studio. He didn't mention anything about the Other Side.'

'He was building an army of zombies!' shouted Alex.

'Don't raise your voice to a superior officer,' growled Tabbris. 'That's insubordination! So where is this army of zombies, then? Hmm?'

Alex's heart sank. 'Cherry made them explode with her singing,' he mumbled. 'Then they, um, sort of vanished.'

Tabbris's scowl deepened. '"Sort of vanished"?' he repeated scornfully. 'How very convenient.'

'But you can ask anyone –'

'Enough!' shouted Tabbris. 'I have no intention of talking to any of these humans. They're already suspicious of us. And you're in enough trouble as it is, without making up fantastical lies about exploding zombies. I might have known your recent behaviour was too good to be true. Well, you can forget about playing in that silly football tournament for a start. I'm certainly going to have a *long* discussion about all this with Gabriel. Now, let's get out of here before we attract any more attention.'

The gang groaned and fell in behind Tabbris as he turned to leave.

'Inchy!'

Jim was approaching them, accompanied by Lily and Mr Kowalski.

'Mr Kowalski says you saved my life,' said Jim, shaking Inchy's hand. 'I don't remember much, but I wanted to say thank you.'

Lily smiled absently and handed Inchy a brown paper bag. 'And I thought you might like these,' she said. 'Something to remember me by.'

'Thanks,' said Inchy, pulling out a knitted bunch of grapes.

'They're better than the ones you got from House, at least,' smirked Spit.

Finally, Mr Kowalski stepped forward and saluted smartly. 'It has been an honour to do battle alongside you,' he said. Then he turned to Tabbris. 'You must be very proud of your grandchildren, yes?'

Tabbris's eyebrows shot skywards. He looked as if he was choking on a boiled sweet. 'Grandchildren? These young insubordinates are no relation to me, sir,' he barked. 'No relation at all.'

'They're angels,' beamed Lily. 'Wonderful, brave little angels.'

'If only she knew,' murmured Spit to Alex, who grinned in return.

As Tabbris turned away, though, the gang were surprised to see Lily's dotty expression vanish. Catching their eyes, she winked knowingly.

'Good luck, little angels,' she whispered. 'You're going to need it . . .'

It all started with a Scarecrow

Puffin is well over sixty years old.
Sounds ancient, doesn't it? But Puffin has never been
so lively. We're always on the lookout for the next big
idea, which is how it began all those years ago.

Penguin Books was a big idea from the mind of
a man called Allen Lane, who in 1935 invented
the quality paperback and changed the world.
**And from great Penguins, great Puffins grew,
changing the face of children's books forever.**

The first four Puffin Picture Books were hatched in 1940 and the
first Puffin story book featured a man with broomstick arms called
Worzel Gummidge. In 1967 Kaye Webb, Puffin Editor, started the
Puffin Club, promising to **'make children into readers'**.
She kept that promise and over 200,000 children became
devoted Puffineers through their quarterly installments of
Puffin Post, which is now back for a new generation.

Many years from now, we hope you'll look back and
remember Puffin with a smile. **No matter what your age
or what you're into, there's a Puffin for everyone.**
The possibilities are endless, but one thing is for sure:
whether it's a picture book or a paperback, a sticker book
or a hardback, **if it's got that little Puffin
on it – it's bound to be good.**